## Everywhere Riley Turned, There She Was.

He was going nuts, and she never even touched him.

He only wished.

The problem wasn't Dori, he told himself. Not her specifically. The problem was *him*.

He was a healthy normal male with all the right instincts—instincts he'd kept reined in for years. Instincts he might have managed to keep well reined in forever if Jake's pretty mother hadn't appeared.

But she had. And she enticed him merely by being there—by cooking and baking and smelling good and smiling at him over dinner at the end of every day.

She and Jake reminded him of everything he'd once dreamed of. Dori, in particular, reminded him of all the things he was missing. And wanted.

Still wanted.

*Bad.*

Dear Reader,

Why not sit back and relax this summer with Silhouette Desire? As always, our six June Desire books feature strong heroes and spirited heroines who come together in a highly passionate, emotionally powerful and provocative read.

Anne McAllister kicks off June with a wonderful new MAN OF THE MONTH title, *The Stardust Cowboy*. Strong, silent Riley Stratton brings hope and love into the life of a single mother.

The fabulous miniseries FORTUNE'S CHILDREN: THE BRIDES concludes with *Undercover Groom* by Merline Lovelace, in which a sexy secret agent rescues an amnesiac runaway bride. And Silhouette Books has more Fortunes to come, starting this August with a new twelve-book continuity series, THE FORTUNES OF TEXAS.

Meanwhile, Alexandra Sellers continues her exotic SONS OF THE DESERT series with *Beloved Sheikh*, in which a to-die-for sheikh rescues an American beauty-in-jeopardy. *One Small Secret* by Meagan McKinney is a reunion romance with a surprise for a former summer flame. Popular Joan Elliott Pickart begins her new miniseries, THE BACHELOR BET, with *Taming Tall, Dark Brandon*. And there's a pretend marriage between an Alpha male hero and blue-blooded heroine in Suzanne Simms's *The Willful Wife*.

So hit the beach this summer with any of these sensuous Silhouette Desire titles...or take all six along!

Enjoy!

Joan Marlow Golan
Senior Editor, Silhouette Desire

Please address questions and book requests to:
Silhouette Reader Service
U.S.: 3010 Walden Ave., P.O. Box 1325, Buffalo, NY 14269
Canadian: P.O. Box 609, Fort Erie, Ont. L2A 5X3

# ANNE McALLISTER

## THE STARDUST COWBOY

SILHOUETTE *Desire*®
Published by Silhouette Books
America's Publisher of Contemporary Romance

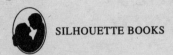 SILHOUETTE BOOKS

ISBN 0-373-76219-4

THE STARDUST COWBOY

Look us up on-line at: http://www.romance.net

**Books by Anne McAllister**

Silhouette Desire

*Cowboys Don't Cry #907
*Cowboys Don't Quit #944
*Cowboys Don't Stay #969
*The Cowboy and the Kid #1009
*Cowboy Pride #1034
*The Cowboy Steals a Lady #1117
*The Cowboy Crashes a Wedding #1153
*The Stardust Cowboy #1219

Silhouette Special Edition

*A Cowboy's Tears #1137

*Code of the West

---

## ANNE McALLISTER

RITA Award-winning author Anne McAllister fell in love with a cowboy when she was five years old. Tall, dark, handsome lone-wolf types have appealed to her ever since. "Me, for instance," her college professor husband says. Well, yes. But even though she's been married to the man of her dreams for over thirty years, she still likes writing about those men of the West! And even though she may take a break from cowboy heroes now and then, she has lots more stories planned for the CODE OF THE WEST. She is always happy to hear from readers, and if you'd like, you can write to Anne at P.O. Box 3904, Bozeman, Montana 59772. SASE appreciated.

For my mother and stepfather,
Ruth and John Perkins,
with thanks for a lifetime of love

# One

Jake Malone was bored out of his skull.

Why should he have to spend a whole sunny June afternoon and half of a perfect star-studded night sitting through a wedding? It wasn't like *he* was the one getting married! It wasn't like he even had to carry the ring or sing in the choir or *do* anything. He just had to sit.

He'd been sitting for hours.

The only other wedding he'd been to—his aunt Milly's last winter—had been pretty cool. And interesting. And short.

Real short.

In fact, it had ended up not being a wedding at all, because right in the middle of the ceremony Cash Callahan, Aunt Milly's old boyfriend, had stopped it. He'd socked the usher who'd tried to stop him—and then Aunt Milly had socked him!

Now, *that* had been worth watching!

It was the reason Jake hadn't minded when his mom had dragged him to this one. Even though she'd said, "Don't get your hopes up," Jake couldn't help it. After all, Shane Nichols, the groom, was usually as interesting as Cash was, and Poppy

Hamilton, the bride, had red hair, and Jake's grandpa always said redheads were unpredictable.

But no old boyfriends of Poppy's had come storming down the aisle. No one had punched anyone else. Shane had been on his best behavior all day, and Poppy had been all smiles. Even Milly and Cash, who hadn't been on the best of terms since that earlier wedding, weren't fighting today.

In fact they were standing in the middle of the dance floor, staring into each other's eyes like they were in some sappy movie. Jake pasted a polite smile on his face, then looked away, disgusted. Nothing exciting was happening at all.

It was so bad that eventually even Shane and Poppy had got bored and left.

"How come they get to go first?" Jake had asked his mother as everyone gathered to throw birdseed and glitter on Shane and Poppy as they escaped.

"It's tradition," his mother had explained.

Jake thought it was time to start a new tradition.

"Mom," he said plaintively. "Can we go now?"

"Not yet, dear." She patted his shoulder, but didn't even look at him. She was shifting from one foot to another in those high heels she almost never wore while she tried not to yawn in Russ Honnecker's face.

Now he watched worriedly as Ol' Boredom Honnecker cranked up the charm. Jake knew his mother wasn't getting any younger, and he supposed she might want a husband. Women did, he'd heard.

But, good grief, *not* Russ Honnecker!

There was no way Jake was going to have Russ Honnecker as a dad!

He snuck out his toe and kind of nudged his mother's leg. She stepped away, nodding at whatever Russ was saying. And nodding. And nodding. Jake thought she looked like one of those stupid dolls with the wobbly heads.

"Mommmmm."

Her hand came down on his shoulder and squeezed. Hard. Jake shrugged away. And then the music started again, and

Jake's mom said, "Why, of course, Russ." And the next thing Jake knew Russ had taken her into his arms.

"Mommmmm!"

She turned in Russ's arms and shot a look like a dagger over Russ's shoulder. "Behave," she mouthed.

Jake glared at her mutinously. Behave? *Behave?* What'd she think he'd been doing for hours? He glared back at her, then swung around and up on his knees to stare out the window into the darkness.

And that was when he saw the cowboy under the streetlight.

Cowboys weren't unusual in Livingston, Montana. Jake saw them in the stores and on the street. He saw them in battered pickups on the Interstate. He sometimes even glimpsed them working cattle when he and his grandpa went fishing up in the valley. He even knew one pretty well. Cash, Aunt Milly's boy-friend, was a rodeo cowboy, or he had been until he'd gone to work for Taggart Jones and Jed McCall. Now he was just a regular cowboy. But that was good enough for Jake.

Jake had been fascinated with cowboys ever since his aunt Milly had taken him to a rodeo when he was two years old. They seemed bigger and brighter than ordinary men like his grandfather, who ran a grocery store, or Mr. Hudson who was retired from the post office and mowed his lawn five times a week, or Russ Honnecker, who was the most boring person on earth.

Cowboys weren't boring.

Except at weddings, apparently, when they were expected to behave, too.

Jake pressed his face to the glass to study the cowboy under the streetlamp. He wasn't at the wedding, so maybe there was hope for him.

He looked just like any other cowboy. Blue jeans. A long-sleeved shirt. Boots. A summer straw cowboy hat shadowed his face from the light above so Jake couldn't see him all that clearly.

He was leaning against the lamppost, one thumb hooked in his belt loop. As Jake watched, he rubbed his shoulders against the lamppost and studied the building where Jake was.

Jake's interest quickened. He felt the stirring of hope.

Was the cowboy one of Poppy's old boyfriends, come to stop the wedding and punch Shane in the nose?

Even as he speculated, Jake's hopes died. Whoever he was, the cowboy was too late for that. The wedding was over; he couldn't stop it. And Shane and Poppy had been gone for at least an hour.

If he was going to punch Shane, he'd have to find him first. And Jake wouldn't be around to see it.

The cowboy rocked on his heels and continued to stare at the building. Once he took a step toward it. Then he stopped and rubbed a hand against the back of his neck. Then he leaned against the lamppost again.

What was he waiting for? Why didn't he just come in?

The cowboy scuffed his toe against the concrete. A tiny arc of sparkly light shot up from his boot. Jake's gaze jerked.

*What was that?* He pressed his face closer to the glass.

The cowboy shoved himself away from the lamppost. Jake straightened, watching intently, waiting for him to come up the steps.

Instead, tucking his hands into his pockets, the cowboy turned and walked away into the darkness. And as he went, wherever his boots touched, a small shower of sparks glittered in his wake.

Jake caught his breath.

Stardust!

It was *stardust!*

He'd seen the stardust cowboy! The biggest and brightest and best of them all—the one his mom had always told him stories about, the one his dad had drawn him a picture of.

"He comes into your life when you least expect it," his mom always said, "and invites you along on great adventures. The question is," she always said, and her voice got deep and round and tempting, "are you brave enough to go with him?"

The cowboy hadn't been waiting for Shane at all.

In Jake's moment of greatest boredom, the stardust cowboy had come looking for him!

He shoved himself off the chair and hit the floor running,

darted between dancers, bumping into them, muttering, "Sorry," as he headed for the door.

Behind him he heard his mother's shocked, "Jake Malone!"

"Come on!" he called back to her. "Come on, Mom! He's here! It's him!"

She'd know who he meant. She was the one who'd told him about the stardust cowboy in the first place. Every night when he was little his mother had held him on her lap and snuggled him close, her voice alive with excitement, as she told him stories of this special cowboy who gives you the chance to live your dreams.

And he was right outside now—if Jake could just get to him.

"Jake," his grandfather called. It was an order. It meant "come here."

But he couldn't obey. Not this time. He pretended he didn't hear and slipped into the foyer. He wrestled with the heavy oak door and finally, desperately, wrenched it open. Then he clattered down the steps, jumping over the last three onto the sidewalk, searching eagerly in the darkness for the sparkle of stardust, for the silhouette of the cowboy who had come to bring him hopes and dreams and promise.

But the cowboy was gone.

Riley Stratton hated weddings.

So standing outside the reception of a couple of people he didn't even know was an irritation right off. They looked so damned *happy.* So fresh and bright and cheerful—as if they had the world by the tail.

Riley sometimes felt as if he had the world by the hooves—and all four were about to stomp him into the dirt.

He had enough to deal with. He didn't need a wedding, as well.

*You didn't have to see it,* he reminded himself. Just because Dori Malone's neighbor had said that's where she was, he hadn't had to come running over.

It was just that he wanted to get it *done.*

He wanted to break the news about his brother, Chris, tell her about the ranch, get her agreement to sell and head home.

That way by tomorrow his life would be back to normal again, and he'd have nothing more to worry about than working his cattle.

And—incidentally—he wanted to see the boy.

The boy.

Riley had stood in the shadows when the wedding guests had come outside and flanked the steps. The bride and groom ran down between them amid a shower of rice and birdseed and glitter. Everyone else had been watching the wedding couple.

Riley had been scanning the guests for a boy.

He'd be close to eight now. There had been several pictures of him in the small bundle of letters that had come last week in the mail. They had been part of what he supposed were Chris's "effects."

Until then it had been impossible to think of Chris as being dead. Impossible to believe that his brother wasn't out there somewhere, driving like a maniac, playing his guitar like an angel, singing up a storm. He'd been gone from home so long—ten years—and had come back so rarely, that Riley had long ago got used to not having him around.

But he hadn't been able to think of his little brother as dead—not even when the very official, notarized certificate arrived from Arizona, where Chris had lived and worked for the past year.

Riley hadn't really fathomed it until he opened the first of the thin bundle of envelopes rubber-banded together and five snapshots had fallen out. Chris, he'd thought at first, because the little brown-haired, blue-eyed boy in the photos looked very much like his brother.

But it wasn't Chris.

Jake was the name on the back of the photos: Jake at four months; Jake's first birthday; Jake at three; Jake in kindergarten; Jake, a gap-toothed seven.

*Who the hell was Jake?*

Scowling, Riley had fumbled the envelopes open and unfolded the letters—first one, then the next, until he'd read them all. There were five, written in a neat feminine hand, and they explained to Riley what Chris never had.

The boy—*Jake*—was Chris's son.

That's when Chris's death had become real.

It was as though, if his brother could have kept such a monumental secret for so many years, he didn't really exist the way Riley had always thought of him, anyway.

And thinking of the vital, vigorous, hell-bent-for-the-horizon, Chris dead and still as the result of a car wreck on a steep mountain road didn't seem any stranger than thinking of his brother as the father of an almost-eight-year-old son.

The more Riley thought about it, though, knowing about Jake made sense of a lot of things Chris had done and said the past few years.

Jake must have been in his mind when, after their father's death four years ago, Chris had declined to sell Riley his half of the ranch. "Nope, I can't," he'd said with his customary blitheness.

"Why the hell not?" Riley had been shocked, unable to understand why Chris would want to hang on to a ranch he'd been desperate to leave ever since he was fifteen.

"It's my legacy," Chris had said. "I might want to hand it on to my own kids someday."

Riley remembered thinking that Chris settling down long enough to marry and have kids was a pretty unlikely prospect. He'd even said as much.

Chris had grinned. "You never know."

Obviously you never did.

Certainly Riley hadn't.

Back then Chris's son must have already been four years old.

Two of the most recent letters thanked Chris for money he'd sent. And that explained a lot, too. Riley hadn't understood why, if Chris was so determined to hang on to his share of the ranch, he'd been so unwilling to plow any of the profits of his share back in.

"I've got other priorities," was all Chris had said.

And all of Riley's scornful comments about Chris's fast-lane life-style had had no effect. All his common sense and logic had been wasted on Chris, he'd thought at the time.

Now he realized that Chris had had other priorities, other obligations.

*You could have said,* he told his brother silently. *You could have told me that you had a son.*

But even as he thought it, he knew why Chris hadn't. His brother would never have admitted to a son he wasn't seeing, a son whose mother he hadn't married, a responsibility that he didn't want Riley haranguing him about.

And Riley would have harangued.

Responsibility, Chris had once complained, was Riley's middle name. "Prob'ly was your first name. They just couldn't spell it."

In Riley's opinion it wouldn't have hurt Chris to have been a little more responsible now and then. In the instance of Jake, apparently he had been.

Sort of.

But he hadn't left a will. It would never have occurred to Chris to leave a will. He'd always considered himself invulnerable, unassailable, immortal. What thirty-year-old believes he's ever going to die?

But he had died. And for almost a month Riley had thought he was Chris's heir. The sole survivor. The owner of the Stratton ranch.

Legally he might be able to pretend he still was. Chris had never married the mother of his son. Marriage had never been a part of Chris's plans.

He was, in his own words, "a rolling stone—lower case."

He was a musician, like the upper-case ones, but the similarity ended there. Chris's music had tended toward cowboy ballads and honky-tonk tunes. A lot of them he had written himself, and Riley knew little enough about music to be impressed.

But what always impressed him more was Chris's determination. From the time he'd been a little boy, Chris had had his sights set on the horizon—on moving out, moving on—and making a name for himself.

''I ain't gonna be no two-bit cowboy,'' he'd told Riley so often that it began to sound like the refrain to one of his songs.

*Not like you.* Chris could never understand why Riley wasn't chomping at the bit to be gone. For years Chris had been counting the days until he graduated from high school and could kick the dust from his boots and head on down the road.

''At least you got as far as Laramie,'' he said when Riley went away to college.

But college hadn't lasted but three years. Their mother died while Chris was still in high school. And right after Chris's long-anticipated graduation and departure, their father had taken the fall from the horse that had crippled him.

There had been no one else to help out—no aunts, uncles or cousins—just him and Chris. So Riley had come home.

Chris hadn't.

''No way,'' he'd said when Riley had finally tracked him down through a series of messages and long-distance phone calls. ''You're not gettin' me back there. You do it if you want, but it won't just be while Dad's laid up. It'll be forever. You're done for,'' he'd told Riley flatly. ''You go back and you're stuck. For good. You're never gonna get away now.''

Riley hadn't cared.

He'd always loved the ranch as much as Chris had hated it. And besides, he'd been fool enough to think that Tricia would come home with him.

Tricia…

*No, goddammit,* he wasn't going to start thinking about Tricia tonight!

He had enough to think about, just contemplating what he had to say to Chris's lover—and to his child.

But he wasn't going to be saying it at any wedding reception. He'd wait until they got home. It wouldn't be that late. A responsible mother wouldn't keep her kid out until all hours. And from her letters, Riley had determined that however big a fool she'd been for loving his brother, in matters of parenthood, Dori Malone was definitely responsible and sensible.

He was glad. It would make telling her easier. And it would make her selling out to him a foregone conclusion.

He tucked his hands into his jacket pockets as he strode away down the sidewalk toward his truck.

They got home just before ten.

Riley had been sitting in his truck down the street from their small two-story house for more than an hour when a car almost as old and beat-up as his truck finally pulled into the driveway.

A woman got out. The other door didn't open, and he wondered for a moment if she wasn't Dori Malone, or if she was, if she had left the boy with someone else. But then she went around to the passenger side, opened the door and lifted out a young boy and set him on the ground. He'd clearly been asleep, and he wobbled against her only half-awake even yet.

A shiver ran down Riley's spine. The boy was *Jake*. Chris's *son!*

He felt a spurt of anger at his brother. How the hell could Chris have just kept on going down the road, never looking back, when he had a child?

Now Riley watched as Jake's mother steadied him with one hand and shut the door with the other. Then, looping an arm around his shoulders, she steered the boy toward the house.

He would wait until she'd put the boy to bed. He wouldn't get to see the kid that way, not up close. But maybe that was just as well. He looked like Chris.

Riley didn't want to think about a boy who looked like Chris. Didn't want to think about having a nephew he wasn't going to have anything to do with.

It wasn't as if the kid knew him, for heaven's sake! Or as if he knew the kid!

It was just that…until he'd found out about Jake, he'd been alone.

It wasn't as if he'd seen Chris much. A handful of times in the past ten years—if that. And it wasn't as if he and Chris had been the best of friends when they were home. In fact Riley remembered spending most of his childhood and adolescence either battling Chris—or battling *with* Chris against someone else, fighting for him, arguing for him, going to bat for him.

When Chris left, Riley had told himself that it was just as well. Life would be a whole lot calmer without him. Chris had been a pain in the neck.

And a whole lot of fun.

Chris had been lightning. Quicksilver. He'd shot through life like a comet—here and there and gone again. Since the day of his birth, Chris had made everyone sit up and take notice. He'd laughed, he'd joked, he'd teased. He'd told outrageous stories; he'd make tremendous demands; he'd sung beautiful songs.

He'd made the whole world laugh and cry—his brother, too.

Riley had never had his brother's charm or his easy smile. He'd marveled at Chris's ability, though he'd never really envied it. Because he knew his brother so well, he'd seen the downside as well as the upside of Chris's mercurial brilliance. He knew Chris's shortcomings as well as anyone.

And he knew his brother's strengths.

Chris would sure as hell not be standing outside some woman's house, waiting for the right moment to knock on her door!

Whenever Chris was anywhere, that *was* the right moment.

*Pull your socks up and get on with it,* Riley commanded himself. He sucked in a deep breath and started across the street.

The front door burst open, and the boy came running toward him.

"I knew it!" he crowed. "I *knew* you'd come!"

Riley froze, gaping.

The boy was Chris all over again. Same dark hair, same high cheekbones, same stubborn jaw. Same quicksilver grin. And he was grinning now at Riley.

Then he yelled back over his shoulder at the woman who was hurrying down the steps after him. "See," he said. "I tol' you!" Then he turned back to Riley again. "What're you waitin' for? Come on in." And he grabbed Riley's hand.

Astonished, mind reeling, Riley allowed himself to be towed. The boy beamed up at him.

"I'm Jake," he said. "But you already knew that, didn't you?"

Well, yeah, but how did the kid know?

Before he could answer, thank God, Jake's mother reached them. It was the first good look Riley had got of Dori Malone up close, and all he could think was, *Trust Chris to pick the most beautiful woman in Montana to be the mother of his son.*

She wasn't his type at all—not the willowy small blond type that Tricia was—but even so, he could appreciate her beauty. She had straight dark hair framing her face, full lips and wide eyes that were a deep dark blue as they stared at him with suspicion. She grabbed Jake by the arm.

"Jacob Daniel Malone! Have you lost your senses? What are you doing, running outside in your pajamas, accosting a total stranger?" She shot a nervous, embarrassed glance at Riley as she tried to detach the boy. "I'm sorry. He's overtired. He ought to be in bed. He's got some notion that—"

"He's the stardust cowboy," Jake broke in. "He *is!* I *saw* the stardust! He was outside the church hall. Weren't you?"

He looked at Riley then, his eyes confident and trusting, exactly the way Chris had always done, knowing his brother would back him up. He was so like Chris. So *exactly* like Chris, it almost took Riley's breath away.

"Weren't you?" the boy persisted when Riley didn't reply at once. "I saw you," he added almost plaintively. For just a second the boy's confidence seemed to falter. "Didn't I?" he asked.

Riley couldn't stand it. He yanked off his hat and raked his fingers through his hair. "You might've. I was...I was there."

Jake shot his mother a triumphant glance. "Tol' ya!"

But at Riley's admission, Dori Malone's eyes narrowed. Then her brows drew down and she very deliberately detached Jake's hand from his arm. "Come along," she said to her son, all frost now as she steered him toward the house.

Riley went after her. "Don't go. I...want to...need to...talk to you."

"I don't think so." Whatever the stardust cowboy was to Jake, she obviously didn't share the boy's enthusiasm.

"My name is Riley Stratton."

It took a second for his surname to register. When it did,

she paled. Then, as he watched, she seemed to draw herself together. She sucked in a careful, steadying breath. "Just a moment."

She turned the boy toward the steps. "Off to bed, Jake."

"But—"

"No buts. It's time for bed. Now."

"Mom!"

"Now."

Jake looked at her mutinously, then at Riley once again. But Riley couldn't help. He glanced at his watch. "It is late," he pointed out.

Jake's face fell. He looked betrayed. Once more Riley was reminded of the way Chris always looked when things didn't go his way.

The realization that he would never ever see Chris look like that again brought a pain so swift and startling in its intensity that he shut his eyes.

"You okay?" the boy asked him.

Startled, Riley opened them again. The boy was still looking at him. But the look of betrayal had been replaced by one of concern. Then Jake nodded, as if he'd come to some decision. "All right," he said quietly. "I'm goin'."

His mother squeezed his shoulder lightly. "That's my boy. Don't forget to brush your teeth. I'll come up and say goodnight after Mr. Stratton has gone."

"And tell me what he said."

Dori Malone rolled her eyes. "If it's any of your business."

Jake looked up, and his gaze met Riley's for a long moment. Then he looked back at his mother.

"It will be," he said.

# Two

The two of them stood looking after Jake in awkward silence.

Then, "Come in," Dori said with a certain resignation. "Whatever you have to say, you don't need to say it on the front walk."

Riley followed her into the house. It was somewhat larger than your basic human chicken coop and reminded Riley of the tiny house he'd shared with five other guys during his brief stint at college. But Dori Malone had done more with it than he and his roommates had. They'd lived with beer cans and beanbag chairs. Here, with worn but comfortable furniture, inexpensively framed family photos, amateurish watercolors and an old oak clock on soft-peach-colored walls, Dori Malone had created a home.

"Sit down. Can I get you a cup of coffee?"

Riley sat, but shook his head. "No. Thanks. I'm fine. I—" He found himself looking at a photo of Jake on the chair side table. The boy was swinging from a tree limb, his two front teeth missing as he grinned a purely Chris Stratton grin. Riley swallowed hard. "He's quite a kid."

"Yes." Dori's face softened as she looked at the photo, too. Then, she straightened and said in a very businesslike tone, "And he's got a bit of an imagination, Jake does. You don't want to pay any attention to it." She gave a slightly forced laugh. "That 'stardust cowboy' stuff, for example. It's just a story I used to tell him."

"Don't worry. I'm under no illusion that I'm a stardust cowboy. You're not going to find anybody with less stardust in his life than me. Dust now—" he shrugged his shoulders ruefully "—I've got plenty of that."

She smiled faintly, and their eyes locked.

Then Dori blinked and went straight to the point. "What's happened to Chris?"

Chris.

Right. Riley took a breath. "Chris is dead. He…died in a car accident in Arizona last month." He watched her as he spoke, ready to stop if she fainted—God help him—but ready to keep going if she'd let him. He just wanted to get it said.

She didn't faint. She sat down abruptly on the couch. What color she'd regained after the surprise at hearing his name, though, fled again at his words. She looked stricken for just a moment, and then something seemed to settle over her—a sense of inevitability, perhaps. She nodded. "I see."

He thought she did. However shocked she might be, he sensed that she wasn't really surprised.

"You were expecting it." It wasn't really a question.

Her fingers twisted. "Not…expecting it. But…" She paused, as if she was searching for the right words. "Chris always lived on the edge. He was…larger than life. Brash. Brave. He…made things happen. Wherever he went he…left a wake."

"Of stardust?" Riley said the words before he thought. "I didn't mean—"

But Dori just nodded and smiled faintly. "Maybe," she said wistfully after a moment. "Once."

The clock struck the hour. Neither of them spoke during the litany of measured chimes. Then, when it fell silent, Dori said, "You're his brother."

Riley nodded. He'd supposed that Chris had told her about his family, even if he hadn't told his family about her. But he didn't know what Chris might have said.

"He talked about the ranch," Dori said. "And about his brother. He made you out to be quite a hero."

Riley felt heat rise on his neck. "Yeah, well, Chris was a storyteller, that's for sure," he said gruffly.

"They were wonderful stories," she said softly. Her eyes got a faraway look in them for a moment. Then her smile faded and she focused once again on Riley. "Did he tell you about Jake?"

"He never said a word. No stories. Nothing." He knew it was blunt, and he wasn't sure it was what she wanted to hear, but it was the truth. Still, he felt obliged to explain. "Chris didn't come back often. Reckon he thought I'd try to make him stay if he did."

*And I would have if I'd known he had a kid,* Riley thought. *I'd have told him to stop fooling around and shape up.*

He hesitated, then added what was only the truth. "I wish he had."

There was a moment of silence, and Riley wondered if he'd said the wrong thing. But finally Dori sighed. "Chris wasn't really into 'family.' And he wasn't especially interested in being a father, either."

*He should have been, damn it.* "He sent money," Riley reminded her. He fully expected her to retort that there was more to being a father than sending money. It was only the truth.

But she didn't. "Yes, he did that. That's something I suppose. And," she added realistically, "maybe it's all he could bring himself to do. Maybe he couldn't come here any more than he could go home. If he had, he'd have had to face up to his obligations."

That was pretty much the way Riley saw it, too. "Did he ever come?"

"No."

"Never?" He couldn't imagine it. Hadn't Chris wanted to see his own child?

"He promised to." She smiled wryly. "'I'll see you at Christmas.' 'Reckon I'll be there for his birthday this year,'" she quoted words that sounded just like Chris. "But, you know Chris." She smiled wistfully. "He promised a lot. He didn't always follow through."

Riley had spent the better part of his life defending Chris's behavior—and being annoyed that he had to at the same time. But there was no defense here—no defense against the truth.

"He meant well." It was the only thing he could think of.

Surprisingly, Dori Malone agreed. "Always." She sighed. "I didn't expect him to come. Not after the first time he said he would and didn't. So I never told Jake he would."

"Does Jake…know about him?"

"He knows his name. He knows he was a singer who was once a cowboy. He knows his father was a man with a lot of dreams." She said the words frankly, without bitterness. Then she smiled. "It was Chris who came up with the stardust cowboy, as a matter of fact. When Jake was two, Chris wrote him a letter filled with grandiose notions about him riding in at midnight and sweeping a little boy up onto his horse and riding off in search of grand adventures, scattering stardust as he went."

Riley smiled. That sounded like Chris.

"My sister had just taken Jake to a rodeo, and he was starry-eyed over cowboys anyway. So when I read the letter to him, he thought it was a story about a cowboy. I didn't tell him it was from his father. He was too little to know what a father was at that point, but he was enchanted with the notion of the stardust cowboy." Her smile got faraway and dreamy as she remembered. "We read that letter so often it nearly fell to bits. And when I did tell him it was from his dad, he said, 'Did the stardust cowboy lead him on adventures?' and I said yes." She looked at Riley almost defiantly. "Why not?"

Wordlessly he shook his head.

"And then we made up more stories—adventures that a little boy might have." Her gaze fell on the picture of Jake that sat on the table. "I don't blame Chris," she said softly, almost to herself. "It's not wrong to have dreams."

"No."

Riley remembered once upon a time back when he'd had dreams—of a home, a family, a pretty little golden-haired wife—before life had got in the way.

He wondered if Dori Malone had had dreams—dreams about Chris. It seemed likely.

Riley could count dozens of girls who'd dreamed about Chris over the years. Chris had always had more women than he knew what to do with—unlike his brother, who'd only ever had one—had only ever *wanted* one. Tricia.

He cleared his throat, put the thought out of his head and straightened where he sat. "Reckon maybe someday Jake can realize those dreams," he said, "whatever they are."

Dori blinked. "What do you mean?"

Riley shifted, feeling awkward, wishing he'd figured out a better way to broach the subject. "I mean he's Chris's heir."

"Chris's heir?" She sounded doubtful. Then she smiled. "Does that mean he gets Chris's guitar?"

"If he wants it." Riley hadn't even thought about that. "It's at the ranch. I can send it. But that's not what I mean. I mean, as Chris's heir he'll have resources so that someday, when he grows up and wants to go to college or do whatever he wants to do, he'll have a stake to get him started."

"Chris had money?"

"Not money. A ranch. *Half* a ranch."

There was a moment's stunned silence. Then Dori said, thunderstruck, "Jake owns half a ranch?"

Riley bounced to his feet and paced the length of the small living room. "It's not all that much. Little over fifteen-hundred acres on the front slope of the Big Horns. Simmental cattle. Not a huge herd. We get by. I do, anyway. It's my life." The only one he knew or was ever likely to know now. "But it sure ain't—isn't—for everyone. So yes, Jake owns half of it, but I'm willin' to buy him out."

"Buy him...out?" Dori echoed.

Riley nodded. "It only makes sense. You could put the money in the bank or invest one way or another. By the time he's grown up, it'd be a pretty good stake for his dreams."

"Half a ranch?" She looked staggered.

"It's not the Ponderosa," Riley said hastily. "Half the time we're damned lucky to break even."

"But you want to buy him out?" She looked at him suspiciously now.

"I'm not tryin' to put anything over on you. I just figured it'd be better this way. It isn't doin' him any good ownin' half of somethin' he doesn't even live near. He'd do better with the money. There's a damn sight more sure things out there than ranchin'. Besides," he added wryly, "lucky kid that he is, he'll likely inherit the whole thing someday."

"He will? Why?"

The weight of a dozen years of loneliness settled down on him. "I haven't got anybody else to leave it to," he said gruffly.

She looked surprised. "No...wife? No kids?"

"No."

"You might have. Someday."

"No." He shut the door hard on that notion. "The place will be Jake's. Trust me."

He wasn't sure that she was going to. She looked a little flabbergasted. He supposed he didn't blame her. She couldn't have been expecting any of this. He sat down again and leaned forward, resting his forearms on his knees. "Look, Ms. Malone—"

"Dori," she corrected promptly.

"Dori," he repeated. Her name felt funny on his lips. Intimate, somehow. He resisted the feeling. He looked at her earnestly now. "It's a good deal. You won't have any money worries. Jake can go to college without gettin' up to his eyeballs in debt. Or if he doesn't want to go to college—like his dad—well, he'll have money to get set up in what he does want to do. He won't be tied down. Ranches tie you down."

Still Dori didn't say a word. She looked as if he'd just punched the air all out of her. "I...need to think about it," she said at last, her voice a little faint.

"Think about it?" What the hell was there to think about? He was offering her thousands of dollars!

"It's so…sudden. I need to…to think," she mumbled.

Well, hell, maybe she did. Maybe she had learned not to be impetuous after her involvement with Chris. He could hardly blame her for that. So he'd just have to swallow his impatience and wait awhile longer. It wouldn't make any difference in the end.

"Fine." He got to his feet. "You think about it. Take your time. And—" he dug into his pocket and scribbled his phone number on the piece of paper tucked in it "—when you're ready, you call me."

Dori stood, too, and took the paper from him. She glanced at it, then set it on the coffee table. "Thank you, Mr.—"

"Riley," he said quickly. If she was Dori, he sure wasn't going to be Mr. Stratton!

She smiled. "Riley." The way she said his name made him feel as if she was tasting it. Tasting *him!*

Cripes! What was wrong with him? He felt heat flood his face. He jerked his gaze away and cleared his throat.

"It was a…pleasure to meet you," he said, his voice ragged. His mother would have been proud. Then he realized that the circumstances of their meeting could hardly come under the heading of *pleasure.*

"I mean, not *why* I met you—" he felt his face burn hotter "—well, you know…"

She smiled slightly. "I know."

The way she looked at him—with those big blue eyes, that soft understanding smile—he wondered that Chris could ever pull himself away. He gave his head a sharp shake and moved toward the door.

He opened it, then stopped and turned back. "Jake's a fine kid. A son Chris would be proud of."

Dori Malone blinked, then she smiled a sad sort of smile. "Thank you."

Riley touched the brim of his hat and went out the door.

There, it was done.

A few days and things would be settled, he thought as he started his truck. He'd made Dori Malone a good offer. Once she'd thought about it, talked it over with her parents or her boyfriend or whomever she trusted, she'd see just how good it was.

She looked like a smart woman. She sure was a pretty woman.

He didn't know why he kept coming back to that!

Well, yes, he did. It was on account of that damned wedding. Weddings made him think about women. And wanting.

But he didn't want Dori Malone.

He still wanted Tricia. Had wanted her for more than a dozen years.

But he was never going to have her. Never.

It was true what he'd told Jake's mother. Since he couldn't have Tricia, Riley Stratton had become a hardened bachelor.

There was no one else to leave the ranch to—besides Jake.

She stood in the doorway and watched Riley Stratton walk down the steps and across the street to his truck. She waited until he got in, started the engine and drove away. It wasn't until his taillights disappeared down the street and around the corner that Dori breathed again and shut the door.

She leaned against it and shut her eyes. Then she wrapped her arms around her body, hugging herself tightly, feeling that, if she didn't, she might just shake right apart.

Chris was dead.

The words were blunt, almost shocking, or—maybe—not so.

The Chris she'd known and thought she loved had, in her heart and mind, died a long time ago. That Chris had died backstage in the Portland auditorium where she'd gone to give him the news. She had suspected, but hadn't wanted to say until she was sure.

But that afternoon the test had confirmed it.

"I'm going to have your baby," she'd told him, curled against the warmth of his chest, confident that once he knew, Chris would rise to the challenge, would welcome the news.

But Chris had gone totally still. And then, slowly, he'd eased her out of his arms. He'd held her away from him and quite matter-of-factly had told her he wasn't ready for parenthood.

"I can't deal with it," he'd told her, as if there was a choice. "It's not part of my plan."

"But—" Dori had begun to protest.

"It won't work. You know. I *told* you. I don't want to get married."

"But—"

"You knew, Dori. You always knew." And then he had told her to go home.

Home? She'd been appalled. She'd left home to be with him. The fight with her father, the hard words, the recriminations that resounded when she'd announced she was going with Chris still rang in her ears.

"I can't go home," she'd wailed.

But Chris had said implacably, "Well, you can't stay here. We travel light. You know that. And if the guys haven't minded sharin' with you, they sure won't feel the same about a baby."

The guys. The band. The band was what mattered to Chris.

"Anyway, I can't talk now. I've got a show in an hour."

The show, of course, had to go on. Dori knew that. She should have realized it before she'd tagged along. His music was what he loved. She was his "girl," his friend, his plaything.

"We have good times" was the way he'd described their relationship.

She should have understood that he didn't want more than that.

She didn't want to go home. But it was the only place she knew of where they had to take her in.

In time she was glad. In time she realized that he had been right. Then she'd been grateful that he'd refused to try to make things work.

They would have ended up hating each other. They would have made life miserable for each other—and for Jake.

It had been better not to have him around. He'd given Jake what he could—Jake's beautiful blue eyes, his dark cowlicky hair, his mischievous grin, his boundless enthusiasm—and the

letter about the stardust cowboy that had fueled his little boy
dreams.

Since Jake's birth she'd never expected more.

She'd never expected half a ranch.

"I own a ranch?"

Dori whirled around.

Jake was standing in the middle of the hallway staring at
her. His eyes were wide and dazed, as if he was waking from
a dream.

Now that Riley Stratton was no longer there, Dori had notions of having dreamed it all, too. "You," she told her son
severely, "are supposed to be in bed."

"Yeah, but—"

"No *buts,* young man. Bed. Right now." She scowled her
best stern-mother scowl. After nearly eight years, Dori was
pretty good at it, even though sometimes she felt like a fake.
Was it because she'd been little more than a child herself when
Jake was born that she felt more often empathetic than dicta-
torial? Possibly.

But no matter how much she might sometimes see the world
as Jake saw it—and dream dreams as fanciful as Jake
dreamed—her job as his mother was to Be Responsible. So she
intensified her sternness and backed him toward the bedroom.

Jake retreated, but as he went, he asked again, "That cowboy...did he say I own a ranch?"

"He said Chris...your father...was killed in a car accident,"
Dori replied sharply.

She was sorry the minute she'd said it. It wasn't the sort of
news one blurted, and she knew it. Jake hadn't known his
father, of course. Not in the flesh. But that didn't mean he
didn't have feelings for Chris.

Sometimes, she thought, the feelings were more pure, more
intense, *because* Jake didn't know Chris.

If he had, he would have had a clearer notion of Chris's
limitations, he wouldn't have put Chris on a pedestal. He
wouldn't be the man for whom that stardust cowboy had come
to stand.

Perhaps it was to break that awe, to demand that he see Chris as a human being who could drive too fast and miss a curve, that she'd spoken bluntly now.

Or maybe, she admitted with more honesty, it was because she felt guilty—because for a split second her attention, too, had been captured less by the pain and waste of Chris's death than by the notion of the ranch that was now his son's.

At her words Jake went totally pale. He swallowed. "Killed?" he said hoarsely.

And Dori felt immediately worse because she realized that Jake's fascination with the ranch hadn't been so great that he'd ignored his father's death. He just hadn't sneaked out of the bedroom in time to hear the first part of her conversation with Riley.

She put an arm around his shoulders, steered him back to bed and tucked him in before sitting down beside him. "I''m sorry, Jake. I''m sorry. I shouldn't have said it…like that."

Jake shrugged narrow shoulders. "'S okay. Just…needed to know."

"Yes. But I should have…been gentler."

"How did he die? What happened?"

Carefully, doing her best not to dwell on the grimmer aspects of Chris's death, Dori related what Riley Stratton had told her. Jake listened, unblinking, until she finished.

Then he waited, not saying anything for a moment, for her to go on. But she didn't, and finally he prompted, "And the ranch?"

She might have known he wouldn't forget about the ranch.

"Apparently your father owned half of the family ranch. As Chris's son, you're his heir."

"What's an air?"

"H…E…I…R." She spelled it for him. "It's what you are when someone dies and leaves something to you."

"The ranch." Jake smiled slightly and settled back against the pillow. "Cool. Not cool that he's dead," he added quickly. "Just…I always wanted a ranch." He yawned then, the excitement of the day finally catching up with him. "I knew it." He smiled again. "I knew it when I saw him. An' then when I saw the stardust…"

"Jake," Dori said sharply. "That's a *story*."

Jake sat up. "I *saw* stardust."

"Describe what you saw."

"He—the cowboy—was standin' by the streetlight watchin' the building, waiting. For *me*."

Dori wanted to tell him not to exaggerate, but unfortunately that part was true. "Go on."

"Well, he just stood there, and he waited. An' waited. And then I guess he changed his mind about comin' in, 'cause he turned to go. An' that's when I saw it! When he walked away I saw stardust, all white and sparkly, scattered behind his boots—a trail. Stardust." And he folded his arms across his chest.

"Glitter, Jake," Dori said, relieved at so simple an explanation. "It was just the glitter we scattered when Shane and Poppy drove away. Remember? We threw birdseed and we threw glitter. That was what you saw. Not stardust. And the man was your uncle. His name is Riley."

A very prosaic name. Nothing glittery about it at all. Just as there was nothing glittery about the man. He was 100% down-to-earth Wyoming cowboy—for all that he was head-turning handsome in a weather-beaten, rugged sort of way. Still, Dori knew that Jake wouldn't notice that—or care if he had.

His attention had been totally captured by the glitter. She looked at him brightly, encouragingly, waiting for his agreement.

Jake just looked at her. "I know what I saw."

Dori sighed. It was useless to argue with him. In the morning, when he'd had time to sort things through, when he was awake and aware, then they would talk about it again. And then Jake would realize that the stardust cowboy was a mythic figure, the hero of a children's story, and that no matter how much you might want him to—he never stepped out of the world of imagination into the real-life world of Dori and Jake Malone.

She didn't believe him.

Well, all right, Jake thought. She was a grown-up. Sometimes grown-ups didn't see what was right under their noses. They needed logic and all that rot to explain things that kids just understood.

Usually his mother was pretty good at that sort of thing. Usually she was right there, sharing when they talked about the stardust cowboy and adventures and dreams.

It was too bad she didn't understand now.

But she would. She'd have to. Because the stardust cowboy had come, promising to take them on a grand adventure. And Jake was ready to go wherever he said.

So what if the stardust cowboy was his dad's honest-to-goodness brother and not the stardust cowboy from the story—that didn't matter. It didn't even matter that his mom had seen glitter where he had seen stardust.

All the dull, logical explanations in the world didn't make a bit of difference because, for once reality was exciting enough to make up for them!

And the reality was that he, *Jake Malone*—a kid who had never done an exciting thing in his life—had all of a sudden, this very night, become the owner of half a ranch!

How could his mother say that Riley Stratton wasn't the stardust cowboy when he'd come bringing news like that?

"Jake!" Dori tapped her foot and glared from the now-cold waffle on his plate to the stairs he wasn't coming down. "Jake!"

Normally every Sunday he was up at dawn—eager and determined and dragging her out of bed to make a "big breakfast" before they went out to play. Sundays, generally the only day she didn't have to work, they always spent hiking or exploring or climbing, all the while telling stories that began "What if…"

Today, of course, was different.

Today she'd agreed to work so her mom and dad could attend a fortieth anniversary party of a couple they'd grown up with. Jake was going to go to Milly's. But Dori had at least made the breakfast. And now he was sleeping in!

"Jake! The waffles won't be fit to eat!"

Finally she heard the sound of heavy thumps coming down the stairs. He appeared, dressed, eyes sparkling, face flushed as if he'd been running, dragging two heavy duffel bags behind him. "I'm packed."

"Packed? What for?"

"Ready to go. To the ranch."

*"To the ranch?"* Dori gaped at him.

He nodded gravely. "When're we leavin'?"

Dori closed her mouth. She swallowed. Her fingers strangled the back of the kitchen chair. "Jake."

*No. Too strong.* She took a breath and forced herself to be quiet, to be calm and rational. To make sense. "Jake, hon'…we're not going to the ranch."

"You mean 'cause you have to work today? I thought maybe it'd be too far. But I wanted to get ready anyway. When can we go, then?"

She forced herself to sound calm and matter-of-fact. "We're not going to go."

"What do you mean, not going? Why wouldn't we go? We own a *ranch,* Mom!"

"For the moment," Dori allowed. "But only for the moment. We can't keep it, Jake."

"Why not?"

"Because…" The word that was the death knell of mothers-in-the-right everywhere. "Because."

Jake looked furious. "Because isn't a reason! You're always tellin' me that."

"Because we're selling it to Mr. Stratton, er, your uncle Riley. He offered to buy it."

"I don't want to sell."

"Well, maybe not. But you need to sell. So you can have the money to go to college or do whatever you want to do when you grow up."

"I want to own a ranch," Jake said stubbornly. "I want to be a cowboy I've *always* wanted to be a cowboy."

*God, give me patience.* "I know you do," Dori agreed. "But you're seven years old, Jake. There's a good chance that you're going to change your mind half a dozen times before you grow up.''

"No," Jake said. "I won't." He folded his arms across his chest. "An' I'm almost eight."

"Jake, you don't know anything about being a cowboy."

"Do, too. Cash told me stories! 'N' Milly did. 'N' you! I know about bein' a cowboy!"

"You know stories."

"Yeah, so? Stories are good! They make you smart. They teach you things. They help you dream. You told me so yourself."

Well, yes, she had. Hoist by her own petard. "Even so, they're just stories, Jake. Not real life. If you still want the ranch when you're grown-up, I'm sure you can go work for him then."

"That's *years!*" Jake protested.

"Yes," Dori agreed, "it is."

"But—"

"I'm not discussing this with you," she said firmly. "I've decided." And she'd spent a sleepless night doing so. "You can unpack all your stuff later. Right now you have to sit down and eat. We're late, and I have to drop you off at Milly's before I head to the store."

For a long minute she thought Jake wasn't going to move. Probably, if he'd been five or six years older—old enough to have heard about passive resistance and sit-down strikes and Mahatma Gandhi—he wouldn't have.

But fortunately he was only seven and three-quarters, and he didn't know all those things. He sat. He stabbed his cold waffle. He muttered, "*I* haven't decided," under his breath. She heard mutiny, pure and simple, in his tone.

But Dori was taking her victories where she could get them: at least he ate.


"You don't need to tell Aunt Milly anything about the ranch," she told him as they climbed the steps to Milly's apartment.

"I can't tell her?"

"No. She'll just…" Well, actually, Dori didn't know what Milly would do. Her steady, predictable sister hadn't been the same since Cash Callahan had crashed her wedding to Mike Dutton a few months before. Before that she'd have supported Dori one hundred percent. But now—now Milly was the proverbial loose cannon. And Dori didn't need her sister's input here anyway.

"Just don't tell her," she said to Jake. "It'll upset her. She'll dwell on it."

Jake banged and banged and banged on the door, so long that Dori thought Milly might have forgotten. But then the door opened a crack and a disheveled Milly appeared. She was wearing a bathrobe, and she looked, well, ravished. She also looked completely amazed to see Dori and Jake.

"What're you—" She clutched her bathrobe around her like she wasn't wearing anything underneath it. Then she must have remembered, because she went bright red and said, "Oh, help! Oh, my gosh. Oh…oh…"

"It isn't Dutton, is it?" a familiar, gruff voice said from behind her.

And suddenly Milly's fire-engine-red color, her clutched bathrobe and her ravishment all fell into place.

"Is that you, Cash?" Dori called.

Jake's eyes went round. "Is Cash here?" he asked his aunt Milly eagerly. "Hey, Cash! Guess what!" He started in the door.

Dori's fingers clamped on his shoulder, holding him where he was. He shot her a despairing look.

He twisted irritably. "I can't *never* tell 'im?"

Dori wanted to say, *No, never.* But his blue eyes were so wide, so eager, so innocent, so full of hopes and dreams. How could you say *never* to a face like that? So she hedged. "Not now."

Jake beamed, then pushed past his scantily clad aunt. "Somethin' great happened. I can't tell you yet," he said to Cash who, Dori was intrigued to notice, was wearing a pair of not-quite-zipped jeans and nothing—obviously—else. "But it's the superest thing! An' you gotta teach me all there is about bein' a cowboy!''

"Jake!"

He sighed heavily. "You never said—"

"It doesn't matter what I said. It's what I meant. And you know what I meant," Dori said sternly. "Go watch cartoons or something while Aunt Milly and Uncle Cash get dressed." She gave them a speaking look. "It is *Uncle* Cash, isn't it?"

Milly's face turned red again. But Cash nodded firmly. "Damn...er, darn right it is."

"Well," Dori said, feeling a little awkward herself as the two lovers exchanged a heated glance. She backed toward the steps. "Congratulations."

"Stay and toast us with a glass of orange juice," Cash suggested.

Dori shook her head. "Can't. Got to open the store. But I'm...very happy for you." She smiled, turned and hurried down the stairs. "I'll pick Jake up about six-thirty," she called over her shoulder, eager to be gone.

"Have fun," Milly said, which told Dori that Milly was still on cloud nine.

Cash was more realistic. "At least keep the brussels sprouts in line."

*Keep the brussels sprouts in line.*

Of course. What else was there to do?

Sorting vegetables—keeping the rotting ones from mingling with the fresh—was just about the most exciting thing in Dori's life.

*What life?* she asked herself as she stood behind the counter and watched Mrs. Campion trundle out the door with her bag of groceries.

Old Mrs. Campion, eighty if she was a day, had more of a life than Dori did.

"Last night I had the most wonderful dream," the old lady had just confided, splotches of red that were not rouge bright on her papery cheeks. "Me and Harrison Ford." She beamed at Dori and fluttered her eyelashes. "It was something."

"I'll bet it was," Dori said.

Dori envied Mrs. Campion her dreams. She envied her Harrison—though he was a little old for her. Once upon a time Dori had dreamed about men, too.

Not anymore.

What was the point?

Dreams were for children like Jake, who hadn't had a chance yet, or for those like Mrs. Campion, who had had a fulfilling life and were now embellishing it with the things they hadn't managed to squeeze in. They weren't for Dori, whose life was mapped out for her.

She'd had her dream. She'd lost it.

Now she had Jake.

It wasn't such a bad trade-off, she reminded herself.

And she had a grocery store. Or she would when her father retired.

"I will," he promised, "when I'm ready."

There was no rushing John Malone into anything. Not retirement. Not stocking new products. Not changing store hours.

Her father believed in stability, continuity, tradition. He was the third generation of Malones to run this store. It had only begun staying open on Sundays when he was in the hospital a couple of years ago after his heart attack. Anything new that Malones carried had been introduced then by Milly who had run things. All the old staples remained. Malones essentially carried the same stock it had carried ninety odd years before.

"Tradition," Dori's father said.

"Tedium," Dori mumbled under her breath.

But it wouldn't have mattered even if she had said it aloud. Her father wouldn't have listened. John Malone heard only what he wanted to hear.

She remembered all too well the incident of the brussels sprouts. Cash, she thought wryly, had chosen his vegetable well.

It had been a simple statement on her brother's part. Deke had been barely twenty-one, chafing under the burden of the store he didn't want to run, eager to pick up his camera and follow his girlfriend to France for the summer. He'd been annoyed that "family expectations" required otherwise, and being told by his father to sort out moldy brussels sprouts was the last straw.

It was nothing; it was everything. In the conflict that ensued, all Deke's frustrations had come boiling up, all John Malone's stern edicts had come pouring out, and by the time it was over Deke had stripped off his stock apron, flung it at his father and walked out.

He had never come back.

Dori had been tempted to follow him.

In those days she had hated the store almost as much as her brother had. And, even more than she'd disliked the store, she'd idolized Deke. And she knew that life without him at home to provide a counterpoint to her father's relentless workaholism would be grim indeed.

And then she'd met Chris. He was the embodiment of Dori's fantasies—a talented cowboy with a beautiful voice and itchy feet, definitely not the sort to appeal to parents. Everyone knew Chris was a here-today, gone-tomorrow kind of guy.

And when he left Livingston, she'd gone with him. Stayed with him. Pretended that everything was perfect. Until she found out she was pregnant and Chris told her to go home.

She'd been terrified to go home. She'd threatened to go off somewhere on her own.

"You aren't that dumb," Chris had said, proving he knew her far better than she knew him. "You won't do anything to hurt that baby."

And she hadn't. Of course she hadn't. She'd loved the child who nestled under her heart even then. She'd slept every night with her arms crossed protectively across her belly.

So she'd swallowed her pride. She'd buried her dreams. She'd gone home.

To her parents. To the store.

To this. A bin full of brussels sprouts.

A future full of them.

*And what's wrong with that?* she asked herself now, tossing a moldy one aside.

The world needed vegetables. Of course it did.

* * *

*"Chris had a son?"*

Riley shrugged, refusing to react to Jeff Cannon's astonished words, hard stare and the sound of his lawyer's feet hitting the floor.

"Yes. And that makes half the ranch his," he said firmly. "I'm buying his share. I just need you to draft the letter, make it legal."

Jeff gave Riley one of his you're-demented-and-I'm-beginning-to-be-sorry-I'm-your-lawyer looks. "The kid's claim isn't legal. It won't hold up in court."

"I'm not cheating Chris's son out of his inheritance." A man had loyalties, responsibilities—even to a nephew he hadn't known he had. "Chris was sendin' money for him."

"Regularly? Was it part of a court order?"

"I don't think so. I didn't ask, but from her letters, it seemed pretty informal…"

"Well, then—"

"Still, he was doin' it. It's why he wouldn't let me plow his share back into the place."

"So you put *your* money in year after year instead," Jeff said sarcastically, "while Chris took his share in profits. And now his kid gets half."

"That's right." He wasn't going to argue about it. His nephew's existence had shocked him, too. He'd even been angry at first, feeling cheated out of the ranch that should have been his.

But now, in a funny way, he was glad. It was good that the kid was there. Now he'd have somebody to leave the place to when he was gone. An heir. A dark-haired, wide-eyed miniature version of Chris. A boy with hopes and dreams and eagerness to spare. A boy like he might have had once if only—

He cleared his throat. His fingers tightened into fists against the tops of his thighs. "It's okay. Don't worry about it, Jeff."

"It's not like you've got stacks of hundred-dollar bills lyin' around. What'd you offer?"

Riley told him.

Jeff's brows lifted, his eyes widened. "Maybe you *do* have hundred-dollar bills lyin' around."

"I figured I could get a loan. I've got decent credit. And I thought if the offer was sweet enough, she'd take it without hagglin'."

"She might reckon she can drive the price up and get a whole lot more," Jeff pointed out.

"No."

"What do you mean, no? You know this woman?"

"Not really." But in an odd way, he felt he did. He'd read Dori's letters to Chris. She'd been appreciative, kind and surprisingly matter-of-fact. And her attitude seemed to require that Chris become a responsible father on some level at least. Apparently her attitude had worked—at least he'd sent her money.

Not that she'd asked for it. Never once had she requested a dime. Not that she couldn't use it. Their little house, clean and neat though it was, was testimony to a life of straitened finances and a determination to "make do."

He was sure the money from the ranch would allow her to move her son to a bigger, nicer place.

"You don't figure you could just take them on as partners?" Jeff suggested. "Like you and Chris?"

"No."

"Why not?"

But before Riley could even begin to explain, there was a light knock on the office door behind him. It opened.

"Ah, Jeff—" The voice was female, soft and melodious, and excruciatingly familiar. " I was in town getting my hair cut and—oh, I'm sorry. I didn't realize you were busy."

"Greta should have told you, Trish," Jeff said gruffly. "Riley and I were just finishing some business."

Trish. Tricia. Tricia Gamble once. Riley's own true love. Once.

Now—and for the past twelve years—she was Jeff Cannon's wife.

"Greta must have gone to lunch," Riley heard her say in that soft, musical tone he remembered so well. "There's no one out here.'' She stepped into the room. ''Oh, Riley.'' She sounded surprised. ''How are you?''

He could smell her perfume. Roses. Tricia had always worn roses.

Now she smiled at him. A gentle smile. A sympathetic smile. ''How are you? Is this to do with Chris? It must be so hard. I just keep thinking about poor Chris…''

She patted his shoulder.

Riley stiffened. She'd hugged him at the funeral. She'd squeezed his hand. He'd smelled the roses then, too, clearer. Closer. Her hair had brushed his face. The fleeting warmth of her body had pressed against his. He turned away from the memory.

''I'm fine,'' he said tightly.

Jeff cleared his throat. ''Maybe you could wait out in the reception area until we're finished,'' he suggested to his wife.

Tricia flashed him a smile. ''Of course. I just came to see if you wanted to have lunch with me?''

''Just give me a few more minutes and we can finish up and let Riley go on his way and—''

''Maybe Riley would like to join us.''

''No, thanks.'' Riley was on his feet before he got the words out of his mouth. He stepped around her, giving her wide berth, moving toward the door. ''I reckon we're finished anyway, Jeff. I just wanted to let you know where things stood and ask you to do that letter for me.''

Jeff rose to his feet, too. ''Trish can wait and—''

''No. She's right.'' Riley glanced at his watch. ''It is near lunchtime. An' I got plenty of work to do.''

''I'll have Greta do the letter after lunch,'' Jeff said. ''I'll send it out to you this afternoon. You can sign it and put it in the mail—if you're sure.''

''I'm sure.'' Riley didn't look at Tricia at all. ''I'll give you a call when they've agreed to the offer.'' He did turn toward her then, touched his hat, and gave her his best, well-brought-up-cowboy nod. ''Nice to see you again, ma'am.''

Tricia's eyes widened at his use of ma'am. Then she blinded him with a smile. ''Always nice to see you, Riley,'' she said softly. Then she touched the back of his hand for just an instant, rubbed her thumb across it.

He jerked back and yanked his hat down hard. "'Bye now."

He was out the door, down the steps and across the street in an instant. He didn't slow down until he reached his truck. There he stopped, with one hand on the door handle and the other—the one she had touched—rubbing the side of his jeans.

When in the hell was he going to stop reacting to her?

She was Tricia *Cannon.* His lawyer's wife. For a dozen *years,* for God's sake, she'd been Jeff's wife!

But one smile from her could still make him quiver, the faintest whiff of her perfume could make his insides knot. And a touch—a simple compassionate gesture, hardly a lover's embrace—could make him jerk away, thinking things he had no business thinking.

Damn.

# Three

Of course Jake couldn't keep a secret forever.

By the time Dori closed up the store for the day and went to pick him up at Milly's the cat was out of the bag.

"A ranch?" Milly squealed the minute Dori opened the door. "You own a *ranch?*"

"Half a ranch," Dori qualified, because there was absolutely no way she was going to be able to deny it. "It belonged to Chris—and his brother."

"Jake told me." Milly's tone lost its excitement and her smile faded as she put her arm around her sister. "I'm sorry, Dor'. About Chris. About…everything. I wish things could have been different for you."

"But then Chris wouldn't have been the person he was." Dori was philosophical now. "He did his best."

"It's wonderful that he left his share of the ranch to Jake. I can't believe you're selling it, though, " Milly said. "Why are you?"

Dori stared. Milly? Asking why she was doing something *sensible?* "We don't know anything about ranching."

"So? You always wanted to learn. You wanted to marry a cowboy, remember?"

"Once upon a time, I wanted," Dori said sharply. "When I was a child, I wanted." And that was a very long time ago.

"Chris was a cowboy."

"Chris was a singer. And I was a fool where Chris was concerned." She looked around for Jake. "Where's Jake? We need to get going."

"He went to Taggart's with Cash." Milly looked just the faintest bit guilty. "They were going riding."

"Oh, for heaven's sake!"

"Jake's always wanted to be a cowboy. Just like you wanted to marry one."

"Just drop it, will you, Milly?" Dori said sharply. But she couldn't seem to drop it herself. "Other little boys want to be firemen and jet pilots and astronauts. But we don't send them out to practice. And they don't end up doing what they think they want to do as children."

"Sometimes they do," Milly replied stubbornly. "Deke did."

"Damn Deke," Dori blurted, shocking her sister. "I didn't mean that." Dori raked a hand through her hair and took a deep breath. "Fine. They went riding. When will they be back?"

"Before bedtime. I'm sure." Milly said, then flushed bright red.

Dori couldn't suppress a smile at her sister's embarrassment. "Right. Cash won't want to miss that," she said dryly.

"I didn't mean—"

"I know," Dori said almost gently, aware of Milly's sensibilities. "But it's about time. You and Cash belong together. Truly, Mil'. I think the two of you will be very happy."

Milly hesitated a moment, then nodded. "I do, too," she said simply. "Now."

Dori knew what she meant. For years Milly's love for Cash had seemed as likely to be successful as Dori's initial crush on Chris. A "here-today, gone-tomorrow" rodeo bronc rider, Cash Callahan had not been given to long-term commitment.

After four years of waiting for him, Milly had finally given up. She'd met and eventually become engaged to someone else.

Her determination to go through with marrying Mike had caused Cash to wake up to what he was going to lose. Unfortunately he waited too long to declare his feelings. It didn't endear him to Milly when he humiliated her by crashing her wedding last winter.

"I love you, and you love me," he'd told her in front of two hundred people.

Whether she loved him or not, Milly hadn't wanted anything to do with him for months.

But last night, at their friends, Shane and Poppy's, wedding, she'd finally recognized that her feelings were never going to change—and that Cash, indeed, was going to stick around.

Now Milly said, "I was scared to trust him after that. And I was angry, too. But I love Cash. I know that now. And—" she sounded slightly amazed "—I actually believe he loves me, too."

"He does," Dori said firmly. She might have doubted it herself once. But she had watched Cash grow up over these past few months. He'd dug in, stayed around, found work and pursued Milly every waking moment. He'd made a commitment, and he'd stuck to it. "You'll be fine," she assured her sister.

"I hope so." Milly gave a little shiver. "This is out of my comfort zone, you know. You always were a better risk-taker than I was."

"Only when Dad goaded me."

"I think you could do it without Dad." She cocked her head and looked at her sister. "I really think you might give this ranch of Jake's some more thought."

No.
Dori told herself that over and over. She'd been telling herself that all last night. She'd told herself that all day.
She told Jake no again, too, when he finally came home saddle sore and eager for more.
No.

But it didn't stop him talking. "It was great, Mom," he said when he wriggled down under the covers that night. "Fantastic. An' Cash says I'm pretty good. He thinks I'll make a hand."

No.

Dori sat on the bed, swung her legs up to sit beside him and reached for the book they'd been reading. It was a Louis L'Amour she'd read herself as a child. It, and many others like it, had fueled her fantasies. Now she wished she was reading him a different story, but she couldn't see how to stop this one and start another without finishing.

"Not this one. Not tonight," Jake said when she opened it.

Dori looked at him, surprised, relieved.

And then Jake said. "I want one of our stories. A stardust cowboy story."

"Jake…"

"Or," he said, his eyes lit with mischief, "I could tell you one. A real one." He flashed her a gap-toothed grin that Dori steeled herself to resist.

"I don't think—" she began, but the flicker of hurt on his face stopped her. He was just a little boy. What right had she to deny his dreams? Life would do it for him soon enough.

"One story," she said. "And *I'll* tell it. Once upon a time there was a little boy…"

She told him the story. She gave the stardust cowboy his due. In fiction, it was his right. But, *it isn't real,* she wanted to warn Jake.

Real life—grown-up life—Dori knew all too well, was brussels sprouts.


"That boy has got blisters on his heels from those damn boots," John Malone said, his brows drawing down as he watched Jake race across the grocery store's small parking lot toward the cowboy who sat waiting in the battered red truck.

"Cash is taking him riding," Dori pointed out mildly.

"He could put them on when he gets there. He's been wearing them all week long."

Dori knew that. Despite her determined refusal to let him think he was going to be a cowboy and move to a ranch, Jake had not given up. He'd put on his cowboy boots the morning after Riley Stratton had appeared on their doorstep. He hadn't taken them off except to sleep. He'd bought a brand-new summer straw cowboy hat just like Cash's with the money in his bucking bronco savings bank. And he hadn't been taking that off, either.

"Damn foolishness," her father muttered. He turned back to the carton of macaroni and cheese boxes he was stamping with price stickers, still grumbling under his breath.

"He's only seven, Dad. It's all right for seven-year-olds to enjoy life."

"You're not helping," he said to her, "encouraging this damn fool ranch notion."

"I am not encouraging any 'damn fool ranch notion'! I'm doing the best I can," Dori muttered under her breath. She grabbed containers of oatmeal that she was shelving out of the carton and changed the subject. "I think we ought to order a few other breakfast cereals. There are new ones on the market, you know."

He ignored her. "His toes'll get pinched in those boots." He punctuated the statement with a stamp on a macaroni box. "And he'll go bald if he wears that hat all the time."

Dori took a deep breath. "What do you think about ordering another granola blend or two?"

Her father glared at her. "I think it's damn fool nonsense! What the hell's wrong with oatmeal? People have eaten it for generations."

"Centuries," Dori muttered. "Nothing's wrong with oatmeal, Dad. It's fine. It's just that some people like a little variety sometimes."

"I don't."

No joke. "We're not all like you."

"More's the pity," John Malone replied gruffly. And Dori knew he wasn't being even slightly ironic when he said it.

"He has the truth," Deke used to say. "And other people have opinions."

"I do things right," her father countered. If he were running it, John Malone always said, "the world would be a hell of a lot more efficient."

"*Hell,*" Deke once said, "being the operative word."

Basically Dori agreed with her brother. But every time she thought it, she was forced to acknowledge two other things as well: *Her father had taken her back when Chris tossed her out. And he thought Jake was the most wonderful person in the world.*

For that last alone, Dori could put up with almost anything. Loving Jake excused a multitude of sins.

"You're not doin' the boy a favor, lettin' him think there's a chance to keep that ranch," her father said now. "Just say no."

"I've said no. But I have to wait and get Riley Stratton's official offer."

Judge Hamilton, Poppy's father, had told her that yesterday, when she'd called to ask his advice on how to do things properly. "You want it on paper," he'd told her. "Always important to have everything on paper."

The paper hadn't arrived yet.

So Jake kept hoping. At least five times a day he looked at her with those big blue eyes and said, "You know, Mom, it'd be okay if you changed your mind." And no matter how many times Dori assured him that she wasn't going to, he always said, "You might."

"I can handle Jake," she told her father now.

He didn't look convinced.


The letter came on Friday morning.

It had clearly been drafted by a lawyer. It was full of proper legal jargon and phrasing. It contained a copy of an abstract as thick as her wrist, and in the end, it made an offer for Jake's half of the ranch.

It was a lot of money. For a long moment Dori just stared at it. Then she thought about all the things that they could do with it. Jake's future was taken care of. She wouldn't have to worry anymore.

Desperation she'd never even realized she was feeling—apparently had been feeling since she'd got pregnant with Jake—suddenly seemed to loosen its grip on her.

Thanks to Chris—she said a silent prayer for the repose of his restless soul—she and Jake would be all right.

It was an unbelievable relief.

Her fingers trembled as she scanned the letter again, then set it aside to look at the abstract. Riley hadn't been kidding. Jake was heir to what, on paper certainly, looked to be a substantial spread. She read details about the herd, the acreage, the number under cultivation, the water rights, the BLM leases, the three-bedroom ranch house, barn and other small outbuildings. For just a moment she tried to imagine it, then shoved the thought away.

There was no point in daydreaming. They had a bird in hand right here.

She picked up the phone and called Rance Phillips's office. Poppy's father had recommended him, even though his office was in Helena.

"I just need someone to check over the contract," she told him.

"No problem," Rance said cheerfully. "We'll check it over and have it back to you next week."

It was that simple.

She rang off and kissed the contract. She felt like kissing the whole world.


Dori wasn't sure Jake would want to celebrate the selling of his ranch, but he had other things to celebrate when he came home from spending a day at Taggart Jones's ranch. He was grubby, sunburned and exhausted when he appeared on the doorstep at six. But he was also grinning all over his face.

"I *helped,* Mom! Taggart tol' me what to do, an' *I did it!* He said I'd make a hand!"

Dori gave him a hug. "Wonderful." She put an arm around his shoulders. "We've been invited to Grandma and Grandpa's for dinner," she said. "Go get some clean clothes. You can get cleaned up at Grandma's."

Jake never stopped talking about the ranch the whole time

he was getting his clothes. He kept talking all the way over to his grandparents' house.

"Guess what!" he told his grandfather, the second John Malone got home from the store. "I herded cattle today. I did good, too. Taggart said so. I'm gonna make a hand."

Dori watched as her father's smile faded slightly. He looked at Dori. "You let him go out there again?"

"He likes it," she said simply.

"It's filling his head with foolishness," her father replied.

*No, it's not,* Dori wanted to retort, but she swallowed the words. Her stormy adolescence had provided enough fights between them. And though she often found herself disagreeing with him silently, her gratitude for his taking her in and accepting Jake had given her the fortitude to suffer their disagreements in silence. His recent heart problems had only confirmed that approach.

So she didn't argue now. But as they sat down to dinner, she said mildly, "He needs something to do in the summer."

"He can come to the store."

"I don't wanta come to the store," Jake said. "It's boring."

"It's life," his grandfather said sharply. "Sit up straight."

Jake sat up straight. He thwacked his fork on the side of his plate.

"Don't do that," his grandfather said. "And don't whine about the store. It's your legacy."

Jake's brows furrowed. "What's a legacy?"

"What you inherit. What you're going to do one day."

Jake brightened at once. "Well, I inherited a ranch! So I'm gonna be a rancher."

"No," his grandfather said, "you're not." Then, ignoring the boy's stricken look, he turned to Dori. "Did you get the contract?"

Dori didn't answer. She was looking at Jake.

He was white. Absolutely white. She had never seen him white before—not when he'd had food poisoning when he was three, not when Buster Keogh, the bully down the street, had sucker-punched him in the stomach when he was five. Not even last fall when he'd fallen off the jungle gym at school and had broken his arm.

He was white—and in pain. And he looked from his grandfather to her—as if she was the only one who could save him.

"Did you?" her father persisted.

Dori dragged her gaze from Jake's face, unable to bear it. "Yes," she answered and heard the raggedness in her own voice. "I did. Today."

He nodded, pleased. "Good. Sign it. Then if you're so interested in catering to the yuppie crowd, you can use some of that ranch money to stock a few new lines. Get some of those granolas you're so keen on."

"Granolas?" Jake echoed.

"Might want to think about reroofing the building, too," John Malone went on. "Reckon we could last a few more years, but it's not a bad idea to do things before they absolutely need to be done."

"Roof the building?" Jake's voice was faint.

"I know it's not my money to be telling you what to do," her father continued, still talking to her, not to Jake. "But it's going to be Jake's someday. You've got to see it succeeds so he'll have something when it's his turn."

"You're sellin' my ranch for the store?" Remote no longer, Jake was almost shouting now. "But I don't *want* the store!"

"Jake!" Dori said desperately.

"I don't! I want the ranch!"

"Someday—" Dori began, trying to placate him, wishing she could just stick a glob of mashed potatoes in his mouth. She did not need another dinner table battle. Not now. Not ever. She'd spent the last eight years of her life trying to make sure it never happened again.

"I don't want someday," Jake wailed. "I got half the ranch now an' I wanta keep it. I don't want that dumb ol' store! Not ever!"

"Jake!" Her father stood so quickly his chair tipped over. And in his voice Dori heard the doomsday knell she remembered all too well. "Go to the bedroom."

For a long moment Jake didn't move. Dori knew he'd never

heard his grandfather speak to him in that tone before, had never had his grandfather look at him that way—as if he'd spoken the unspeakable when he'd dared express what was in his heart.

Dori reached beneath the table and gave his fingers a squeeze.

He looked at her.

But she couldn't help him. Not now. "Go on, Jake," she said quietly.

His lips came together in a thin line. His eyes went glassy and flat. Slowly he pulled his hand out of hers, got to his feet and turned away from the table.

Then he stopped and looked back—at her. It was a look she'd hoped never to see—a look of betrayal.

"It's my ranch," he whispered.

Dori started to reach a hand out to him, but her father said firmly, "That's enough, Jake. Go. Now."

Jake went.

The silence that settled over the table echoed with the bitter words of a thousand confrontations. Deke's and her father's. Hers and her father's. Storms and recriminations. Anguish and harsh words.

Gone, Dori had dared hope, forever. But they weren't gone. They'd come again to strike another generation.

Then, "Pass the meat loaf," her father said.

Her mother passed it. Held it out to Dori to hand on to her father.

Dori didn't move. She sat in the eye of a hurricane, the emotions of a lifetime whirling around her.

Her mother reached past her and handed it on. Then she patted Dori's hand gently. "He's just a little boy, dear. He'll learn what really matters."

"Damn right he will," her father said gruffly. He helped himself to the meat loaf and forked another piece onto Dori's plate, as well.

She stared at it. Bile rose in her throat. "I'm full," she said. "I don't want any more."

Her father poked a fork at her. "Don't insult your mother's meat loaf."

"Have some brussels sprouts, dear," Carole Malone said. "You know you like them."

*He'll learn what really matters.*

"Eat," her father said. "I didn't hurt him. He'll get over it."

*He won't.* Dori knew he wouldn't. She picked up her fork. It was all she could do not to gag as she ate.

Riley had never been so tired in his life.

He'd been moving cattle from sunup to sundown all week, doctoring pinkeye, doing some vaccinating, fixing some fence, cursing the hot dry weather that seemed to invite his calves to try their swimming talents in whatever bogs they could find.

It seemed like he spent all day hauling them out and moving them, only to find them bogged in the following day somewhere else. It was not his idea of a picnic.

He dragged himself toward home Sunday evening, eager for a long hot soak, a heated-up frozen dinner and eight hours of uninterrupted sleep, after which he was definitely going to find himself a hired hand.

Last year Chris had come home long enough to help him during the busy times. This year there was no Chris.

There was no one but him.

According to Jeff, if Riley actually bought Jake out, there wasn't money to hire a hand, either. According to Jeff, there wasn't going to be money for much of anything. But Riley had gone ahead and made the offer, anyway.

Once he had made up his mind about something, that was that.

He'd find the money somewhere, he'd told Jeff. There were plenty of useless things in the house he could sell.

"Junk," Jeff said.

"Well, yeah. But hey, I reckon it's all in the eye of the beholder. What's junk to you and me might well be somebody else's antique."

Jeff had been doubtful, but Riley persisted. He'd sorted

through piles of stuff that he hadn't used in years, and when he'd gone into town to pick up the letter Jeff had drafted for him, he'd stopped at the paper and told Sherry to put an ad in.

"It'll run in Sunday's paper," Sherry had told him.

Now he urged his horse into a trot as he came over the hill, then hauled up on the reins as he saw a car with a trailer attached parked next to the ranch house.

"Well, I'll be damned." He rubbed a hand against the back of his head and grinned. "How 'bout that?" he said aloud. "I told Jeff they'd be coming out of the woodwork, an' he didn't even believe me."

He touched his spurs to his horse's sides and started down the slope. A child came around the corner of the barn and spotted him.

"There he is!" the kid shouted. "He's comin'!"

The door to the car opened and a woman got out.

Riley was pleased. A woman was more likely to buy junk and think she'd got a deal than a man was. He tried to muster up a smidgen of cowboy charm.

Then the kid came running toward him, grinning and yelling—a kid with cowlicky brown hair and a gap-toothed grin that Riley recognized about the same instant he heard the words.

"Hi, Uncle Riley. Guess what! We're movin' in!"

# Four

She hadn't expected Chris's brother to be thrilled. But she wished he wouldn't look quite as poleaxed as he did.

Granted that the twilight didn't show colors to their best advantage, he could have at least managed a little in his face as he rode toward them. In fact, Dori thought Riley Stratton looked whiter than chalk as he reined in his sorrel and stared down, first at Jake and then at herself.

She rubbed her hands down the sides of her jeans and pasted her best cheerful-shopkeeper smile on her face. "We decided not to sell," she said.

His brows drew down. "You what?"

She shrugged awkwardly, hating her nervousness, hoping she didn't betray it to him. "We decided not to sell," she repeated, slower this time in case he simply hadn't heard her.

But from his darkening expression, she knew he had. "I sent you a letter," he said. "A contract. You were supposed to sign the contract."

"Yes. I know. It was…very generous. But…well…Jake doesn't want to sell."

*That's right, Dori. Blame it on your child,* she thought, disgusted with herself. "*I*...don't think it's right for him to sell," she corrected herself.

"Why the hell not?" Riley Stratton's voice was harsh.

Dori glanced quickly at Jake, hoping he didn't pick up on the anger in his uncle's tone. They'd heard enough anger recently.

But if he did, he didn't show it. Jake was as matter-of-fact as ever. "'Cause I want to be a cowboy," he said simply, looking up at his uncle. "I know you tol' Mom I'd get the ranch eventu'ly, but I don't want it eventu'ly. I want it now if it's already half mine. That's why we're here. That's why we're movin' in."

Riley sat absolutely still astride his horse. He looked absolutely stunned.

Apparently Jake thought so, too, and decided that more of an explanation was called for. "We didn't come to mooch," he told his uncle earnestly. "We come to help. I been learnin'. All week. I went and rode with my uncle Cash. An' I helped Taggart, his friend, move cattle. They both say I'm gonna be a good hand," he announced proudly.

In the still-stunned silence that followed, Dori prepared to react. If Riley Stratton said one negative word to Jake, she'd go for his throat and she knew it. She'd had enough sarcastic negativism to last her a lifetime.

That was—really—why they were there.

Her father had trampled her dreams eight years ago. She'd agreed to it, had known it would happen when she'd come back home. It was the unspoken price her father had exacted for taking her in. It was a price that, under the circumstances, she'd willingly paid. She'd have gone on paying it forever.

But she wasn't going to let him trample on Jake's.

When she'd seen her son's eagerness fade, his smile vanish and his shoulders slump, when the light in his eyes had gone out and his future seemed to contain nothing better than an endless stream of granola boxes and brussels sprouts, she'd known what she had to do.

But she didn't imagine that Riley Stratton was going to agree.

Now he looked down from his horse at her small son and said, "Of course you are." He smiled a tired, but real smile at his eager nephew. "You're a Stratton, aren't you? We're all damn fine hands."

And Dori felt like throwing her arms around his neck and giving him the biggest kiss imaginable.

Fortunately, before she did anything as foolish as that, he looked back at her. "I don't understand."

"You will," she assured him, breathing easier, breathing deeply, and smiling—smiling all over her face. "I promise. You will."

He'd never seen a woman smile like that.

Not at him, anyway.

It was blinding. Astonishing. It damn near knocked him off his horse.

No, what had damn near knocked Riley off his horse was a whole different kind of astonishment. *What the hell did the kid mean, they were moving in?*

*You can't,* he'd wanted to say. *No way,* he'd wanted to say. *Over my dead body,* he'd almost said.

But how could you say a thing like that to a boy with such hope—and desperation—in his eyes.

Chris's eyes.

*Sucker,* Riley chided himself. He rubbed down his horse, taking his time, trying to figure out how to handle this, knowing even as he did so, that control of the situation was escaping him, that even as he stalled, they were setting up camp in his house.

Like he'd ever had control at all, he thought grimly.

Even now he could hear sounds of them moving up and down the front steps, hear the front screen door banging open and closed. They were *moving in.*

And how was he supposed to stop them?

Tell them to go away?

He couldn't. He didn't have the right.

But he'd never thought they'd want to move in!

*You should have thought of that when you made the offer,* Jeff would say when he found out. And then he would doubt-less grin and say, *Well, at least you've got enough money to pay a hired hand now.*

Maybe they wouldn't stay.

Yeah. Riley stopped brushing his horse. He stood quietly, letting the words sink in, testing them, probing them. Yeah. Maybe they wouldn't. *Probably* they wouldn't. They were town people. Town people liked lights and action. They liked to be able to go out to restaurants and to see films. They liked being able to pop over to the neighbors for a cup of sugar. Little boys in town liked to ride bikes with their buddies down the street.

There were no streets here. No bikes. No restaurants. No lights. No action. Not even any neighbors for better than five miles.

People who weren't born to ranching couldn't stand it. Even some people who were couldn't stand it, he remembered. Like Tricia.

He couldn't see Dori Malone and her kid lasting long.

He breathed a little easier. He could put up with company for a little while. It wouldn't last. It was just a matter of waiting them out.


The ranch house kitchen was old-fashioned, its pine-paneled walls were weathered with age. The burners on the old stove, which ran on LP gas, had to be lit with a match. But Dori found matches, and she washed one of the several pans soaking in the sink—obviously Riley was no fan of doing dishes—and heated up a can of soup. That would take the edge off the hunger Jake had suddenly decided was killing him. Then she set about paring potatoes to go with the steak she had brought in the cooler. She was a little worried that Riley would think she was trying to take over, and she hoped a good meal would be a peace offering.

"No brussels sprouts," she murmured as she fixed the potatoes. As far as she was concerned, there would be no more brussels sprouts in their lives as long as she lived.

Jake was eating the soup, the potatoes were boiling and Dori was up to her elbows in dishwater—washing what looked like a week's worth of Riley's dishes—when the back door opened and the man himself stepped into the kitchen.

On horseback Riley Stratton had looked imposing. In the kitchen, in his socks, she'd imagined he'd be less so.

Somehow he wasn't.

Chris had never daunted her, had never made her swallow and take a step back—or if he had, it was only because he was so darn good-looking.

But Riley was daunting. He was no taller than she remembered Chris. Neither was over six feet. But Riley was filled out. His shoulders were squarer, his chest deeper. For all that he was as lean as Chris, he seemed more muscled and less slender. His hair was darker and shorter than his brother's had been, his features sharper, his jaw more uncompromising, his whole aspect harder, less handsome—and more intimidating.

Dori ran her tongue over her lips and took a quick, steadying breath.

Riley didn't speak. He stopped dead just inside the door, his hand still on the knob, as he looked first at her standing by the stove and then at Jake seated at the table.

Jake, as usual, rose to the occasion, looking up, grinning through his tomato soup mustache. "Want some dinner?"

"He was hungry," Dori apologized quickly. "We hadn't eaten in hours. And it isn't yours, the soup I mean. I brought it with me." She didn't mean to sound so defensive, but somehow she couldn't seem to stop herself.

Riley blinked. Then he said, "You're welcome to whatever food you find." There seemed almost to be a line of color rising in his face. "There ain't—isn't—much. I haven't been to the store in a while."

"I brought plenty of groceries." Dori waved a hand toward the sacks she'd lined up on the counter. "I expect to pull my weight. We can share."

"Share?" Riley looked at her, baffled.

"The groceries. The...house."

He didn't reply. The silence was deafening.

Then quite suddenly she heard a soft rumbling sound coming from the region of his stomach. She frowned for just a moment, then grinned with relief when she realized what it was.

Riley instinctively pressed a hand against his belly. A touch of color definitely crept into his cheeks now.

"Sit down." Dori waved a hand at a chair, as if it were her kitchen, not his. "You must be starving, too," she said. "The soup is ready. The potatoes will be soon. I brought some fresh green beans. The steak's almost ready." She turned to look for a clean bowl to dish him up some soup, then remembered they were all in the sink.

Riley obviously realized this, too, as the color in his face deepened, and quickly he shook his head. "You don't need to fix me anything."

But in the silence after he spoke, his stomach growled again. Dori laughed.

"Really. I don't expect—"

"You obviously weren't expecting *us*," Dori cut in. "We've landed on you without any warning at all. I apologize for that. It couldn't be helped. At least let me begin to make it up to you by fixing dinner. Do you need to shower first or do you just want to sit down and eat?"

He seemed almost nonplussed for a moment, then he said, "Um, shower. I need a shower."

"Everything will be ready by the time you get back," she promised.

He started down the hallway when she spoke. "Riley?"

He looked back over his shoulder.

Dori gave him the best smile she knew how. "Thanks."

She made his dinner.

Soup. Steak. Mashed potatoes. Green beans. His stomach thought he'd died and gone to heaven. It was the best meal he'd eaten in...well, *years* maybe. Certainly the best one he remembered.

He said so.

The tomato soup was out of a can, she told him, holding it up. "I just added a little dill, and I made it with milk."

He supposed that was what made the difference. He didn't know. She'd probably done something equally prosaic to the potatoes, too. But they tasted better than any he'd ever had. And the green beans. He poked at a brown speck in them.

"Bacon bits," Dori explained. "If you don't like them, I can leave them out next time."

Next time? There was going to be a next time?

He didn't know how he felt about that. But did he like them? "Hell—I mean," he said with a nervous glance at Jake, "heck, yes."

She smiled at him again. "Good. I'm glad. I'll be happy to do all the cooking."

"Er." He took another bite and chewed. And chewed. To give himself time—to fathom, to cope, to think. He'd thought that he'd be able to sort things out in the shower, but he hadn't. He'd stood there with the hot water sluicing down over his body, and he'd remembered the way Dori Malone had smiled at him, and he'd found himself reaching out and turning the tap to cold.

She'd rattled him.

Since Tricia, no woman had rattled him.

It was because he was tired. He'd been working too hard. A good night's sleep and he'd have a better grip. She wasn't *that* pretty. And she wasn't blonde. He preferred blondes.

He swallowed. "Well," he managed after he took a long gulp of milk. She'd brought that, too, guessing rightly that he wouldn't have had any in the house. "I don't know. We can try it for a while, I guess." The cooking, he meant. Until she got tired of the place and left, he meant.

He wished she wouldn't smile at him like that.

Not when he didn't have a cold water tap handy, at least.

"Can I get you some more?" she asked him. "There's more potatoes. Another piece of steak?"

He started to say no, but then he thought it wouldn't be near as good cold tomorrow. He nodded and shoved his plate toward her. "Sure. Why not?"

She brought him more steak, more potatoes, more beans. She made coffee and poured him a cup. Riley ate all the food, cleaned his plate completely, then settled back, sated, in his chair and cradled the cup in his hands.

She made good coffee. A damn sight better than the coffee he made. Chris said he couldn't believe anyone would drink Riley's coffee.

"It's swill," he said. "Pigs wouldn't drink it."

Riley had never noticed. He didn't think he was a connoisseur of coffee, but even he could tell the difference between what he made and this. He balanced the cup on his broad gold belt buckle, stretched his feet out in front of him and crossed them at the ankle.

A guy could get used to this.

And the very thought had him sitting up straight and slapping his cup down on the table so hard the liquid sloshed all over the oil cloth. He had no intention of getting used to anything of the sort!

Dori turned from where she was rinsing plates at the sink. "Something wrong?"

"Yes. No," he corrected hastily. "I just…thought of something." He shoved himself out of the chair and stood up. "I got…book work to do," he improvised.

"Oh. Of course. Don't let us stop you." She hesitated, then said, "But I wonder if you could tell me where to put Jake's things. He's getting a little tired."

"Am not," the boy said, though he was sitting at the table, one hand propping his head up. He blinked furiously to look wide-awake.

Riley, watching him, almost smiled. Then he thought about what she'd asked him, thought about where the heck he was going to put them for even the brief period they managed to remain.

"Come on," he said to Jake. "You can have our old room."

"Whose?" Jake asked, his brows arching in curiosity.

"Mine and your dad's. It was the one your dad always used when he came home," he added. It felt funny talking about Chris as anybody's dad, let alone this boy's. But it was true.

And it still boggled Riley's mind every time he thought about it—just like it boggled him that Chris had never bothered to meet his son. "This way."

He picked up the duffel bag that Jake said had all his "special stuff," then led the boy—and his mother—down the hall and into the smaller bedroom. The bunk beds he and Chris had slept in were still against the far wall. The desk their dad had built was under the window. There were pictures from their high school days. A poster from a twenty-year-old Cheyenne rodeo still hung on the wall. Nothing had changed—not even the paint—in years. Riley was embarrassed to think how shabby it must seem. Their place, tiny though it had been, was at least freshly painted and clean.

But Jake only saw one thing. "Wow. Cool! I always wanted bunk beds! Can I sleep on the top?"

And his mother, who, Riley was sure, saw all the shortcomings that her son didn't, just looked at Riley. "Can he?" She grinned. "You have no idea how many years he's been clamoring for them."

"He can sleep wherever you want. There're clean sheets in the closet. I'll get 'em." He pulled a set out and Dori took them from him. He started to help her make the bed, but it felt somehow far too intimate, and his hands dropped to his sides.

"Don't let me keep you," she said quickly.

"Huh?"

"From the book work."

"Oh, right." He scratched the back of his head. "Yeah." He glanced from her to the boy. Both of them were smiling at him. He managed a quick, almost desperate smile in return. Then "G'night," he said over his shoulder and fled.

He retreated into the alcove off his own bedroom. It had been "the babies' bedroom" when he and Chris had been in diapers. When they'd moved across the hall into the room where Jake was now, his father had turned the tiny alcove into "the office." It was a glorified term for a desk, a filing cabinet, a slipping tower of stockman's journals, stacks of graph paper breeding charts and a brand-new computer, which Riley was doing his best to come to terms with, determined that by learning to use it, he would be able to chart the herd better, have more information at his fingertips and, thus, make more well-informed decisions.

He wondered just how well-informed the decision was to buy the damn computer sometimes. But he assured himself he would get the hang of it—if he ever had the time.

Now he had time.

He was well fed, through no effort of his own. He wasn't going back into the kitchen which suddenly seemed "Dori's territory"—not for anything on earth. And he'd just lied and said he had book work to do, hadn't he? Well, surely book work could be expanded to include learning this blasted software program for herd management that he'd purchased.

So he turned it on. Then he sat there, stared at it and tried to figure out what he was doing.

The computer program was no more mysterious than his life.

He couldn't focus on bales per ton or tons per month. His eyes drifted past weight at birth and gain per ton of dry matter fed. It was gibberish to him. His mind tried to bend it around, get a grip on it. He could get Dori Malone and her pint-size cowboy out of his head.

And then he heard light footsteps behind him, and he jerked around.

Dori stood there, a tentative look on her face. "I'm sorry to interrupt. I was wondering… Jake would like to say good-night to you."

"I already said good-night."

"Yes," she agreed. "But he didn't."

Riley hesitated, feeling awkward. But then he shrugged and got to his feet. Dori looked past him toward the computer screen.

"Book work?" she asked.

He grimaced. "If I ever get that far. It's a new computer. A new program. And an old cowboy." His mouth lifted in a wry twist.

She smiled. "Not so very old," she said.

The way she looked at him made his whole body warm. Or

maybe it was just hot in here. Yeah, probably the start of a damn summer heat wave.

He stepped carefully around her. Seeing Jake seemed suddenly less awkward than staying here.

The boy was tucked into the top bunk—Riley's old bunk—his trademark eager grin on his face, his arms folded behind his head. "Dylan has bunk beds," he said. "But when I sleep over, he always gets the top one. Here, I do!"

"Who's Dylan?"

"My best friend." Then Jake's grin faded. "Back in Livingston he was my best friend, anyway. Maybe he won't be my best friend now that we've moved."

*Maybe you'll have moved back by then,* Riley thought, but he didn't say it.

"Oh, I reckon you're probably friends for keeps," Riley said to him. "You look like that sort of guy."

Jake's grin came back again. He looked pleased as he leaned up on one elbow. "Then maybe before school starts he can come visit?"

Riley wasn't sure how to reply to that. "Depends on what your mother says." That seemed safe enough.

Jake settled back against the pillow. "It doesn't matter. What matters is that we're here. Even though I saw the stardust, I was afraid Mom was still gonna say no."

"There wasn't any stardust," Riley told him, wanting to get that straight.

Jake raised his shoulders slightly. He smiled.

"There wasn't."

"Mom said it was glitter," Jake told him. He didn't sound like he cared.

"That's right," Riley said. "Glitter. And manure and dust," he added. There was no point in romanticizing things.

"Yep," Jake said. It didn't seem to matter at all. "Cash—my almost uncle—says he reckons the stardust cowboy can come in lots of forms."

It was like rowing upstream at flood stage. "You get some sleep," he told the boy. "Reckon you're pretty tired."

"Kinda," Jake admitted. He snuggled down under the blankets, then reached out a hand, offering it to Riley.

Riley hesitated for just a second, then took it in his. It was small and mostly soft, but along the palm Riley felt a line of new calluses. He ran his thumb over them.

"From when I was at Taggart's," Jake explained. "Learnin' how to cowboy." The boy's eyes—Chris's eyes—met Riley's with eagerness and trust. His palm lay open in Riley's big rough one. Then he turned his hand over and gave Riley's a squeeze. "I still got a lot to learn. But you'll teach me, won't you? I mean, we're partners now, aren't we?"

Riley swallowed. He blinked. Then he nodded slowly. "We're partners."

Dori stood staring at the computer screen. It contained a database not unlike the one that Milly had developed for the store. The categories were different, but the principles had to be the same.

It was the one really nice thing about computers as far as Dori could see. They followed patterns. If you put the right numbers in the right slots, you got the right answers. It was simple.

Very unlike life.

She rubbed her hands on the sides of her jeans and tried to steady her still-hammering heart. It had settled down pretty well during the time she was fixing dinner. *She* had settled—probably because fixing meals was part of the autopilot behavior that got her through life. It was soothing, regular, an everyday activity where the ease of long practice took over.

What would happen when Riley came out of Jake's bedroom would be exactly the opposite.

She'd had no practice at all trying to explain what had to seem to him totally irrational behavior. She wasn't sure it *wasn't* irrational behavior. She just knew that she had no other choice.

Well, he would have to understand. She would *make him understand*.

"So tell me what's going on."

She hadn't heard him come back in the room. At the sound of his voice right behind her, she jumped and spun around. He stood there, hands loose at his sides, but still ready. He reminded her of a gunslinger, balancing on the balls of his feet, all senses at the alert—waiting for the explanation he had every right to.

Dori cleared her throat. "Why don't we…go into the other room." The alcove where she'd been standing was right off a bedroom that was clearly his. Granted that the whole house was his, still it seemed smarter to get on more neutral ground.

Wordlessly Riley shut down the computer and then waited for her to precede him out of the room.

But if she'd thought that the right words would come the minute they were back in the living room, she was wrong. There didn't seem to be anything she could say that would make him nod and say, "Of course I understand. It makes perfect sense. I'd have done the same thing."

He tapped his sock-clad toe on the floor and waited, unblinking.

Dori shrugged helplessly. She sat on the edge of one of the overstuffed chairs and knotted her fingers in her lap. Then she looked up at him. "I know you expected us to sell. *I* expected us to sell. But in the end…I couldn't."

Still he didn't speak. He just looked at her.

"We had to leave," she said at last. "If we hadn't my father would have killed Jake's dreams."

She didn't know she was going to say it until the words came out of her mouth. And then she thought, *Yes, that's basically the truth.*

"It was all right that he killed mine," she added with determined honesty. "It was fair. I…deserved it. But I couldn't let him kill Jake's!"

She expected him to tell her she was exaggerating. But he didn't. He just propped his butt against the fireplace, folded his arms loosely across his chest and said quietly, "Tell me what you mean."

So she did. She talked about how desperately Jake had always wanted to be a cowboy, how living on a ranch had always been his dream. She rambled, she was sure, but he didn't stop her.

And his undivided attention gave her courage, and she kept right on. She told him about Jake buying the cowboy hat with his savings. She told him about Jake wearing the boots every day and getting blisters, about how he'd never once complained—or stopped wearing them. She told him about Jake's eagerness to go to Taggart's, and even when he was tired and battered and sore the first day, to want to go back. And back. And back.

"He's always wanted to be a cowboy," she said, her eyes locking with Riley's. "He was doing everything he could to make it happen."

And then she told him about the night of the meat loaf dinner.

"If you'd seen his face when my father said we could sell the ranch and start a new line of breakfast cereals. I couldn't let him take Jake's dreams and destroy them." She lifted her gaze and met Riley's desperately, blinking fiercely against the tears that had been threatening to fall ever since she'd determined to leave Livingston.

"I couldn't sell. I had to give him a chance, don't you see?"

Riley saw.

He didn't want to, but he did.

He stood in the yard outside the bunkhouse in the darkness and stared out at the sky and tried to muster up a reasonable argument that would refute everything Dori Malone had said.

But he couldn't—because he understood.

He understood desperation. He understood dreams.

He remembered having had his own share as a child. He'd had more as a young man.

When he was a boy he'd dreamed of cowboying, too. Then of owning his own ranch—*this* ranch—along with Chris, and following in the footsteps of his dad. When he was a young man, Chris had already opted out, but Riley had kept his basic dream and added to it. He'd found the woman he wanted to marry then. And he'd dreamed of bringing her back—of marrying her and growing old with her and passing on the ranch to their sons who would have grown up by his side.

Oh, yeah, he'd had dreams. Just like Jake did.

And then his father had been hurt, and Riley had come home to take over. Tricia had stayed at college. "I'm going to college to get out of there," she'd told him.

He'd thought she would change her mind. They'd been going together for years. He'd loved her forever.

The following year she had married Jeff.

"Jeff's in law school," she'd said when she'd announced her engagement to the son of Jim Cannon, the Stratton family's lawyer. "He's got *plans*. He isn't going to be any two-bit rancher for the rest of his life."

"I thought you loved me," Riley had argued.

"I do love you," Tricia had told him. "I just hate the ranch. Leave the ranch and I'll marry you."

But he couldn't leave. He couldn't leave the old man in the lurch. He didn't *want* to leave, anyway. "I thought you understood. You always knew I wanted to come back."

"And you always knew I didn't."

Maybe he had. Maybe he'd just never thought she meant it. Maybe the ranch had mattered so much to him that he'd just assumed she'd come to feel the same way.

"Please, Tricia," he'd begged. "I love you."

She'd kissed him.

But she'd still married Jeff.

Sometimes Riley thought he'd got the last laugh when, six years ago Jim Cannon had had a stroke and had asked his son to move home from Denver and take over the practice.

The knowledge that Tricia had had to come back pleased the tiny wellspring of bitterness that lurked in the back of his mind. *Serves her right,* he'd thought when he heard.

She'd crushed his dreams. Now hers had been crushed, too.

It was a sentiment he was ashamed of, one that he certainly wouldn't admit to anyone. And one that he quickly came to regret.

For if Tricia had suffered for the past six years, so had he.

He'd done all right putting her out of his mind while she

was hundreds of miles away down in Denver and he saw her only once in six years.

Now he saw her several times a month. Now when he called Jeff at home, she answered the phone. He got to hear her voice. It still teased him, tempted him, taunted him.

Now he reckoned God had the last laugh on both of them.

Fair enough. But what the hell was God doing bringing Jake and Dori Malone into his life?

Giving Jake half the ranch when he legally wasn't required to was supposed to be his good deed—the fair and honorable thing to do. The deed that would let him sleep nights and grow old and go to heaven when his time came, even if he turned out to be a crotchety old bachelor whose name was used to scare the local kids.

It wasn't supposed to bring them to his doorstep.

It wasn't supposed to send him off to sleep in the bunkhouse.

"You don't have to do that!" Dori had said half an hour ago, sounding scandalized when he said that's where he was going.

"No place to sleep in here. You can have my room," he'd told her.

"I'll sleep in with Jake."

But he'd just pointed her toward the clean linens and grabbed a sleeping bag for himself. "I've got to be up and out early. I'd wake you."

"We didn't come to put you out of your house!"

But he hadn't listened. He'd left.

And now he stood outside the bunkhouse, his sleeping bag under his arm, and looked up at the stars.

There were a passel of them out here where no city lights reached. He was used to them, saw them so often he didn't pay much attention anymore. Now he did. They were scattered across the heavens…like stardust.

His gaze dropped, seeking the upstairs window of his old bedroom—the bedroom where Jake now slept. He noticed that the curtain had been pulled back.

Was that Jake in the window?

Jake. In his mind's eye Riley saw the boy's infectious grin, his Chrislike eyes, his cowlicky hair. In his heart he knew Jake's dreams. He didn't blame Jake's mother for wanting to preserve them for him.

But would the ranch do it? Or would the ranch turn his dreams into a reality he wanted no part of?

Well, if it did—that was life.

They thought he was asleep, but he wasn't.

Sure, he was tired. Anybody would be tired when they'd spent all day helping sort and pack an apartment full of stuff nd load it all into a trailer, then got up five times last night to look out the window just to be sure the trailer was still there.

His mom had told him she'd changed her mind. He'd heard her tell his grandfather that they were going to keep Jake's share of the ranch after all. And it wasn't that he didn't believe her. But he'd seen the way she'd looked when she did it, the way her knuckles were white as she'd knotted her fists at her sides, and the way her voice sounded sort of thick and achy, like her throat was sore.

He'd seen, too, the look on his grandfather's face.

Mom and Aunt Milly sometimes called Grandpa "Old Grumpy." But Jake had never seen it until that night.

"I'm quitting the store," his mom had told Grandpa. "We're keeping the ranch. I want Jake to have a chance."

And Grandpa's face had gone white, then red, and he'd stared at her like she'd done something terrible, like she'd shot his best horse. Just the look had made Jake's fists clench and his stomach hurt. He'd wanted to stop it.

"Mom, we don't have—" he'd begun.

But she'd stepped between him and his grandfather. "Yes, we do," she'd said. Her voice had been quiet, but her words had been firm.

Still Jake hadn't been able to imagine it happening.

So he'd got up again and again, to check and see if the trailer was still there, needing to make sure it was really going to happen. And every time he did, he'd looked at the scattering of stars in the sky and thought of the stardust cowboy, then he'd closed his eyes and prayed with all his might.

Now he leaned his chin on his fist on the windowsill and looked at those same stars. They were bigger, he thought, and brighter here than they ever looked in Livingston because it was so dark out here. There were no streetlights here, no headlights, no neon signs. No lights at all except the one behind the curtains at the front of the house.

They were here. At the ranch.

If he turned his head and looked around the bedroom, he could see outlines of pictures that he knew were of his father as a gap-toothed boy no bigger than him.

Outside, if he looked down he could see the outline of his uncle Riley, big and tall and strong as his dad would have been, standing in the yard looking up at the stars.

Jake remembered the first time his mother had taken him outside to look at the stars. It wasn't nearly as dark as this, and there hadn't been as many stars—but the ones that were, she told him, were powerful. They connected people.

"What's c'nnected?" he'd asked her.

She'd linked her fingers with his. "It's like this," she'd told him. "You and I are connected because our fingers are hooked together. Stars can hook people together, too, because we can each see them from so far away. Like now," she said, "your daddy's in Texas, but he can see those same stars."

"He can?" Jake hadn't known how far away Texas was in those days, but just the sound was foreign.

"Mmm," his mother had murmured. "I just got this story in the mail. A…friend wrote it. Let me read it to you. It's about a stardust cowboy."

And that was how it had begun. She'd taken him inside and had read him the story—about the cowboy, about the stardust, about adventures. Later, much later, she'd told him his father had written it.

Jake could remember the end of it now. *Always look out in the sky at night and know he's there. He comes when you least expect him, to sweep you up into life's most wonderful adventures.*

Jake's lips moved silently as he said the words to himself now. His dad had written it to him, his mom had told him later.

"He wants you to think of him," she'd said. "And to know he's thinking of you. You're connected by the stars, you see."

Jake didn't know if his dad could still see stars from where he was in heaven, but it seemed like a pretty good bet. He lifted his gaze to the scatter of stardust that seemed brighter than ever tonight. In the distance he heard a horse whinny and he heard Uncle Riley's boots go up the bunkhouse steps.

"I'm here," he said quietly. "At your ranch. In your old room. An' if you're listening," he said to his dad, "I just want to say thanks."

# Five

He thought they'd get fed up.

Certainly there was nothing much fun or romantic or inspiring about mending fence or doctoring cattle or baling hay. The hours were long, the sun was hot, the cattle were stubborn, the haying was a necessary evil. Riley detested it. Jake seemed to thrive.

He was up bright and early every morning, raring to go.

The first morning Riley had expected it. He'd been prepared—although relatively red-eyed and sleep-deprived from his night on the moldy mattress in the bunkhouse. He'd been determined to give Jake a good day's work—not to overdo things, but to let the kid get an honest sense of what he was in for.

"A partner's gotta pull his weight," he'd told Jake when showing him how to saddle the horse Riley had chosen for him.

"I'm ready," Jake said. "Let's go."

"Are you sure you want him tagging along all day?" Dori had asked. She'd been up, too, fixing them a breakfast like

Riley had only dreamed about since his mother had died fifteen years ago.

"I'm sure. It's his ranch, too."

Something had passed between them then—an acknowledgment on Dori's part of what he was doing—not making it easy for Jake, but making it real. Not trampling the boy's dreams, but letting him test them against the reality of the ranch.

"Have a good day," she'd said.

They did. In spite of the fact that Jake slowed him down, got in his way and dropped things, Riley found he liked having the kid around.

The boy was endlessly curious. He asked a thousand questions, but he didn't chatter idly. When Riley answered, he went silent, digesting what he'd been told. Only when he had another question did he speak again—or when he had an observation to make.

It was the observations that Riley enjoyed even more than the questions. The questions allowed him to explain what *he* knew. The observations allowed him a glimpse into his nephew's eager mind.

"Grandpa says he likes his steaks better in the butcher's case than on the hoof," he told Riley that first day. "Not me." He'd lifted his face to the sun and smiled. "I like 'em out here where the wind is blowin' and I feel free."

"Me, too," Riley agreed. He had never understood Tricia's fascination with cities. They smothered him, made him crazy. He liked space. He liked to be able to see the horizon, to go a long, long time without seeing people.

Except he didn't mind seeing Jake.

In Jake he saw bits of Chris—the Chris that Chris had always been determined not to be. He wondered that the boy was so much more like his uncle than like his father. He wondered if Chris would have been irritated that the boy liked the ranch. Probably Chris would have been amused.

"Reckon he's a throwback," he would most likely have said, and then he would have fixed Riley with a devilish grin. "Like you."

Riley knew that in Chris's eyes he had always been something of an anachronism—"a nineteenth-century cowboy trying to make it in a twentieth- and twenty-first-century world." And learning about the computer was his way of trying to straddle both. But he couldn't help being pleased that Chris's son seemed to feel the same way he did.

The kid worked as hard as he did, too.

Riley kept a close eye on him, wanting him to experience how much there was to do, but at the same time, wanting to be sure the kid didn't drop from exhaustion.

He shouldn't have worried.

Jake was a go-er, a worker, a doer. He'd been stiff and sore and sunburned when he staggered out to meet Riley the second morning. But when Riley said, "You want to give it a miss?" the kid shook his head emphatically.

"I'm a partner, aren't I?"

He was that.

They spent a week together—almost every daylight hour—now. And Jake was not just hanging in there any longer, he was getting stronger, harder, tougher, smarter. He didn't need Riley's help as much. He could saddle his own horse, muck out stalls, throw a rope and, sometimes at least, catch something. He could drive the pickup, if Riley put a pillow on the seat so he could see, and he knew enough to leave the open gates open and keep the closed gates shut.

At the end of that first week, they circled up to check on the cattle near the area where Riley and Chris used to swim when they were kids. It was a kind of natural bend in the river that had been cut off when a new channel cut a shorter loop. The swimming hole left behind was where their dad said he'd swum, too, as a boy.

Jake's eyes got wide when Riley suggested a swim. "You mean it?" He was off his horse in a flash, sitting on the ground and tugging at his boots, eager to jump in. Then his face fell when he realized he didn't have any swimming trunks.

"It's what underwear is for, didn't you know that?" Riley said. "So you've always got a swimmin' suit when you need one."

"Is that what you're gonna do?"

"Of course." Riley didn't mention the times he'd gone skinny-dipping here with Tricia when they were in college.

Some things a guy needed to grow up and figure out for himself.

"Last one in's a rotten egg!" Jake shouted and streaked toward the water. He plowed in, shrieking when he encountered what was little warmer than snow-melt. But it didn't deter him. He dove under and came up sputtering. "Come on, Uncle Riley! What're you waitin' for?"

Riley kicked off his own boots, shirt and jeans, and dove after Jake.

They splashed and played and laughed until Jake's lips were blue and Riley's teeth were chattering. Then they scrambled out and Jake wondered what they were going to do about towels, so Riley showed him another use for a good sturdy shirt.

"It's all wet then," Jake grumbled when he finally had to put it back on.

"Well, I reckon if it bothers you, you won't be wanting to come back anymore," Riley said with a grin.

Jake looked at him, astonished. "Not come? Of course I'm comin'. I'll just keep a towel in my saddlebag from now on. Next time can we bring Mom?"

"Er." Riley's mouth went suddenly dry at the thought.

As much time as he happily spent with Jake, he spent as much time avoiding Jake's mother.

Not that he didn't like her. He had no reason not to like her. She was up every morning before he was, putting together both breakfast and lunch so they'd have something "to start them out," as she'd told Jake, and something "to keep them going," as she'd said when she'd handed Riley packets of sandwiches and fruit and home-baked cookies that she said were "not all for Jake."

"I'll share," Jake had said, offended. And he'd made sure he did, though Riley had protested that he didn't need any cookies.

"You don't like 'em?"

"I didn't say I didn't like 'em," Riley muttered, backed into a corner. He didn't lie. He just didn't want to be beholden.

"You gotta eat 'em then, or she'll think you don't," Jake advised. "It would hurt her feelings."

So Riley ate them. Well, hell, he couldn't hurt her feelings.

She had dinner on the table every evening, too. Wonderful dinners. Roast chicken. Steak. Stuffed pork chops. Green chili stew. Salads with fresh vegetables Riley had never met before—at least not in that form.

"That's spinach?" he'd said doubtfully when she'd identified the dark green leafy vegetable mixed with the slices of red onion, mushrooms and chunks of hard-boiled egg. "I thought spinach came in a can."

After that she called him Popeye with a teasing light in her eye that for some reason made his neck feel warm and his face flush.

"You don't have to feed me so much," he'd told her gruffly when the meals came day after day. "My jeans are gettin' tight."

At the waist, he meant. The *waist!*

But when she'd looked at him and her gaze dropped, it hadn't seemed to stop at his belt buckle!

Cripes! Riley turned and beat a retreat toward the bunkhouse as fast as his legs would carry him.

"I got work to do," he'd said over his shoulder. "I got to mend some tack."

He'd done his best to stay out of her way after that—making up excuses not to watch the television program in the evening that Jake wanted him to watch—"all of us together." He didn't need that sort of togetherness.

Didn't want it.

It would remind him all too forcefully of what he'd once hoped to have with Tricia. He did his best not to let himself think about that.

So he told Jake, "I got work to do," a lot, too. And if he didn't hightail it out to the bunkhouse or the corral to work on the horse he was gentling, he holed up in the alcove and tried to make sense of the damned computer.

He wasn't kidding, either. Trying to deal with that computer was damned hard work. Harder than anything else he did all day—and not just because of the pain-in-the-neck software program, either. It was that he had to go through his old bedroom—now Dori's—to do it.

Nothing had changed, he told himself. It was the same old furniture—the same blue walls, the same drab curtains that had always been there. And that was true, as far as it went.

But somehow he felt like he was invading the quarters of some mysterious harem. He hadn't ever lived around ''women stuff.'' His mother had been the most discreet of women. He didn't ever remember seeing her underclothes lying around.

But Dori Malone's were.

Of course—he'd kicked himself when he realized it—she had no place to put them. The dresser was full of his stuff. So he moved it all, jammed some of it in the bottom two drawers of the dresser, threw the rest in a duffel and took it with him out to the bunkhouse.

He figured that would solve the problem. But it didn't. Next time he ventured in on his way to the alcove, there was a filmy nightgown hung casually over the back of the chair. There was a stack of colored brief panties on top of the dresser. He jerked open the drawer to see why the hell she hadn't put them away, and was confronted by half a dozen wispy lace bras next to a bunch of perfectly prosaic T-shirts.

She wore underwear like *that* under her T-shirts?

He could hardly look at her again without his eyes going straight to her breasts. Then he'd find himself running his tongue over his lips and swallowing hard.

Somehow he'd thought Tricia was the only woman in the world who ever wore sexy underwear.

It had bothered him for a long time that she was taking off that underwear for Jeff and not him. But somehow it bothered him just as much that Dori Malone was wearing underwear like that and not taking it off for anyone!

And then there was her perfume.

It wasn't like any other perfume he'd ever smelled. It wasn't like flowers or musk or any of those things that other women

wore. It wasn't the pale scent of lilacs that he'd always asso-
ciated with his mother—and it wasn't that hint of roses that he
remembered all too well from nuzzling his nose against Tricia's
neck.

No, this was sneakier.

It crept up on a guy when he wasn't paying attention. It
nailed him when he was just walking past her in the kitchen
or helping her change the oil in her car. It was—hell, he didn't
know what it was. It was sweet, it was spicy. It was purely
Dori Malone. And being within four feet of it was driving him
nuts.

"You like puttin' that stuff on by the gallon?" he'd asked
her one afternoon when he passed through the kitchen and
somehow caught a whiff of it while she was folding laundry.

"Stuff?" She'd looked at him, baffled. "What stuff?"

"That perfume."

"I'm not wearing perfume," she told him. "Maybe it's the
fabric softener," she suggested. "I use it to get rid of the static
cling."

And damned if she didn't hold up a pair of his very own
snowy white briefs to demonstrate that they weren't clinging!

Well, that particular pair wasn't. Riley reckoned he might be
somewhere close to scarlet. "What the hell are you doin' with
my underwear?"

"Folding it. Don't I fold it the way you want it?"

He was supposed to have a preference on folding underwear? He snatched them out of her hand. "You don't need to
bother."

"It's no bother," she protested.

But it was. To him, oh, yes, it was! "Forget the laundry,"
he said gruffly, grabbing up all of his that he could see, bar-
ricading himself behind it as he held it in his arms.

"I need to do something," she told him. "I said I'd pull my
own weight."

"You are pullin' your weight," he told her. "You cook, you
clean."

"I do laundry," she said archly, "when I'm allowed to."

He shifted from one foot to the other. He scowled. His arms clutched the laundry close.

"I'm trying to help," she said patiently, as if he were a not-too-bright child who needed these things explained. Or a not-especially modern man who didn't like strange women pawing his underwear.

So, maybe he wasn't a modern man! But Dori Malone wasn't his mother, and she sure as hell wasn't his wife—and something in him just knotted all up at the thought of her smoothing her hands over his shorts.

Now if she'd been Tricia...

But she wasn't Tricia. There was no hope for Tricia. She was untouchable. A married woman. He had to stop thinking about her.

It was Dori Malone's fault that he was.

Before Dori had shown up, he hadn't spent every waking minute missing Tricia. Most days he didn't think about her at all. He got on with his life, with his work, with improving the ranch—trying not to think about the dreams he'd dreamed, the hopes he'd once had.

But now he thought about them. A lot.

Because of Dori. Because of Jake.

They'd been here a week. Jake was still as gung ho as ever. Did that mean they were really going to stay?

What the hell was he going to do if they stayed?

What was he going to do if they didn't?

He'd got used to having Jake as his shadow. He liked having the boy around. Even if he wasn't a son, he was a nephew. That was the next best thing.

Too bad he came with a mother.

It was Dori—and all she reminded him of—Riley could have done without.

*Well, happy trails to you, too,* Dori thought as she watched Riley striding away from her toward the bunkhouse, a mountain of unfolded laundry in his arms.

What on earth was that all about?

Dori couldn't figure him out.

At first she figured that despite his politeness about their having landed on his doorstep, he was really not happy to have them there. But as the days passed, she'd had to reevaluate that notion. He seemed perfectly happy to have *Jake* there. He spent every day—*all day*—with Jake, and seemed to enjoy it.

It was her he was avoiding.

So what was he, one of those aw-shucks-ma'am-cowboys like *The Virginian,* a guy who talked to his horse and had never said three words to a female of the species in his entire life? Or was he a misogynist, a man who didn't like any women at all?

She debated asking him. Dori was usually straightforward, accustomed to shooting from the hip. But somehow she didn't think that was a good idea with Riley. Not now. Not yet.

Maybe when she knew him better.

*And when is that going to be?* she asked herself. At the rate they were going, they might exchange a thousand words a year.

"Does he talk to you?" she'd asked Jake one evening when she was tucking him into bed.

Jake's brow had furrowed. "Talk to me? Who? Uncle Riley? 'Course he talks to me! He tells me about the cattle an' the ranch an' stories about my dad. Why *wouldn't* he talk to me?"

"No reason," Dori said. She smiled and gave a quick, dismissive shake of her head. So it wasn't that he didn't *ever* talk. It was just that he didn't talk to *her.*

No, that wasn't true, either. He did talk to her. He told her *not* to do things.

"Don't wash my clothes. Don't fold my clothes. Don't go to so much trouble making cookies. Don't leave your, um, clothes on the dresser anymore. I cleaned out some drawers for you."

Well, that had been nice of him.

He was nice to her. Polite to her. And he kept his distance from her.

*You wanted him maybe to snuggle up?* she asked herself.

The question, coming right out of the blue like that, jolted her. *Snuggle up?* Where on earth had *that* come from?

She didn't want any such thing! She wasn't angling for romance from Riley Stratton, for goodness' sake!

Talk about complications!

But the words plagued her, and Dori was self-aware enough to admit they contained a grain of truth. It wasn't romance. It was awareness.

She wasn't used to being a woman ignored.

She'd never before thought of herself as requiring attention from members of the opposite sex. But perhaps that was because she'd always *had* attention from members of the opposite sex.

Chris certainly hadn't been the first.

As far back as she could remember, boys had paid attention to her. They'd teased her and talked with her and stood on their heads trying to impress her. They *liked* her.

She was cute, her friends told her. She had "personality." She made every boy feel like he was special, Milly told her. Dori didn't know what it was she did. It just came naturally to her. She had just always liked people—all people—and she let them know it.

She'd had her pick of boys since junior high.

Chris had been the first one she'd ever been serious about. He was the only one she'd ever slept with, despite having tried to shock her father by making him believe otherwise. But even after Chris, when she'd narrowed her sights considerably and had rarely even chosen to date, it wasn't because guys weren't asking her.

*Lots* of guys asked her. All of them liked her. All of them talked to her. All of them had let her cook dinner for them.

She was willing to bet they'd have even let her fold their laundry.

Not Riley Stratton.

Stubborn cuss of a man!

Well, fine, if that's the way he wanted it, he could do his own laundry. She would find other ways to help out.

She went into town the next afternoon.

She hadn't been to town since they'd passed through on their way to the ranch the day they'd arrived. She needed to pick up some groceries. She wanted to stop by the school and register Jake for third grade in the fall. And she was going to buy material to make new curtains for the kitchen and for Jake's bedroom.

The nearest town was fifteen miles distant. There wasn't a lot to it—one main street and a couple that crossed it. Besides Jeff Cannon's law office, there was a gas station and convenience store, a small grocery, a hardware store-cum-welding shop, two bars, a restaurant, a jail-turned-historical-society-and-museum, a post office and a Laundromat.

So much for that, Dori thought wryly when she saw it.

She drove on past and headed toward the small brick school on the edge of town. In summer, of course, there were no classes, but she'd dated a teacher for a while when Jake was small, and she knew that teachers and administrators were often at school when there were no students to be found. If no one was there, she could come back. If someone was, she would introduce herself and maybe find out about any local children Jake's age.

There had to be some times when Riley would be glad not to have a shadow dogging his every step. He'd been incredibly tolerant so far, but she couldn't expect him not to want some time to himself. And Jake did need to develop friends his own age.

The building was open, but there was no one in the office when she went in. Still, she could hear talking in the distance, a woman's voice and at least a child or two, so she pressed on.

At the far end of the hall of classrooms, she found an open door and looked in.

A slender woman with deep auburn hair was talking to two equally redheaded children. They started to move a bookcase and she looked up, noticed Dori and smiled. "Oh, hi. Have you been there long? Are you lost? Can I help?" She set the bookcase down again and came toward Dori, holding out her hand. "I'm Maggie Tanner. I teach third grade."

Third grade? Then she might be Jake's teacher. Dori took her hand and returned the smile. "I'm Dori Malone. My son and I have just moved here, and I came to see about registering him for school.''

"You need to see Jeannie to do that," Maggie Tanner told her. "She's the secretary. Or Betsy, the principal. Neither one of them is here today. We just came in to do a little rearranging. These are two of my boys, Seth and Nick. They're in second grade."

Dori shook hands with each of them, and then said, "Jake, my son, is going into third."

"Then he'll be mine," Maggie Tanner told her. "I have the only third grade here. I have my own son, Jared, too, next year." She laughed. "That ought to be interesting. He's out helping his father today on our ranch. But I told Robert I needed help, too, and so I commandeered these two."

"You have three boys?" Dori was pleased to hear that. At least Jake might be able to make friends with them.

"Yes. And a daughter, Lissa. She's four. Tell me about Jake. I didn't realize anyone new was moving into town. Word tends to travel pretty fast here, as you might imagine."

Dori smiled. "Jake is out cowboying, too, today. With his uncle. Riley Stratton."

Maggie stared at her a moment, then she shook her head. "Riley's his uncle? Then he's…"

"Chris Stratton's son," Dori said, lifting her chin. Maggie Tanner didn't look like the sort of woman who would pull back in disgust, but Dori really didn't know her at all. And this *was* Chris's hometown. Who knew what people thought of him here?

But Maggie didn't bat an eyelash. "I was very sorry to hear about Chris," she said gently. "I didn't know him well. I didn't come here until after he'd left. I only met him a couple of times when he came back to visit or to help Riley out during branding or roundup. He seemed very nice. But—" Maggie's gentle smile widened "—we all love Riley. He's the salt of the earth, Riley is. He'd do anything to help—anyone, anytime, anywhere. He'd give you the shirt off his back."

*Not if it was dirty, he wouldn't,* Dori thought.

"Yes," she said aloud. "He's been…very kind."

"Are you going to be...staying with Riley?" Maggie's tone was speculative.

"We're staying on the ranch," Dori said. "Jake inherited his father's half."

At that Maggie's eyes did get large. "Oh," she said. "My," she said. "Well, imagine that," she said. There was a little hint of color in her redhead's complexion. "We never realized... I mean, I'd understood there wasn't a will. We all thought Riley—" She stopped. The color was high in her cheeks now. "I have a big mouth and a small brain," she said. "Forgive me."

Dori felt quite suddenly as rattled as Maggie Tanner. Chris *hadn't* had a will? He *hadn't* left his half of the ranch to Jake?

She shook her head. "N-no. I mean, yes. Of course. There's nothing to forgive. It's...it's just...we were as...as surprised as you must be," she managed after a moment.

"Well," Maggie Tanner said briskly, "I, for one, am *delighted* you're here. I will be thrilled to have Jake in my class, and overjoyed that my three musketeers will have someone new to play with. And I'm especially glad for Riley."

This last was added with an intensity that brought Dori up short. Maggie Tanner was glad that Riley had, presumably, just *given away* half of his ranch? She tried to make sense of that. She couldn't.

She would have to ask Riley—she would damned well ask Riley—when she got back to the ranch.

"We'll have to have a party," Maggie went on, oblivious to the thoughts reeling through Dori's head. "To welcome you and Jake. To celebrate!"

"Oh, I don't think—"

"There aren't a lot of people out here," Maggie went on firmly, "so we all need to know each other and stick together. It's important." She fixed Dori with a steady gaze. "I'll talk to Robert tonight, then call you and Riley and let you know when." Dori suddenly found her hand clasped between both of Maggie's. "This is wonderful news," Maggie said, giving Dori's hand a squeeze, and there was no doubting her sincerity. "We're so very glad you've come."

*   *   *

She couldn't talk to him in front of Jake.

She never saw him any other time!

She needed to talk to him now! At once! Immediately!

All the way back to the ranch, she fretted. All during the cooking of dinner, she fumed. All the while they were eating, she studied him openly, trying to figure him out. But he didn't glance her way. He studied his plate, his food, his nephew. But he didn't so much as look at her while she carried on wondering, worrying.

After dinner she tried to ease Jake away from his side long enough to ask him about what Maggie had said. But Jake had a million questions. And Riley had plenty of answers. Answers that took them up until Jake suggested they watch a TV program, and then Riley glanced at his watch and muttered something about work he needed to do, and promptly vanished out the back door.

She couldn't go after him. Not then.

But once Jake was asleep…

*She* wouldn't sleep until she'd demanded—and received—an explanation.

Had he really simply *given* Jake half the ranch? Had Chris had nothing whatever to do with it at all?

And, most important, if it was true, *why?*

Maybe Maggie was wrong. Maybe there had been a will. Maybe she and Jake weren't there under false pretenses.

But if Maggie was right, that was very much what it sounded like.

# Six

The knock on the bunkhouse door startled him.

"C'mon in," he called. He was lying on the bed in his shorts, reading a Western, and thinking how much easier those nineteenth-century guys had it with only vigilantes, hired guns and the Johnson County War to worry about.

Now he shoved himself up against his pillow, glad for company, pleased that for once Jake had decided to come visit him instead of urging him to stay up at the house and watch TV with them.

"Got bored with that ol' TV, did y—" Riley began as the door opened. Then, "What the hell are *you* doin' here?"

It wasn't Jake who stood in the doorway.

Riley took one look at Dori, standing there blinking at him in his undershorts, and scrambled up, scrabbling for his jeans, holding them in front of him.

"Out!" he said. "Wait out there!"

"I need to talk to you," she replied, not moving. At least she had the decency to look away, to pretend he wasn't standing there within inches of being naked right in front of her.

"Fine. We'll talk. Now get outa here. Lemme get dressed!"

"You said come in."

"And now I'm sayin' get out. Please," he added.

She scowled, but at least she left. She went outside and pulled the door shut after her.

Geez. Riley let out a shudder and yanked his jeans on, then zipped them up. He snatched a clean shirt off a hook on the wall, and dragged it on, then buttoned it and stuffed it into his waistband.

He pulled on a pair of socks and shoved his feet into his boots. There. He might have wished for a suit of armor, but this was better than what he'd been wearing.

"Come in," he said. He made his voice sound steady by sheer force of will.

The door opened a crack. "Are you sure?" There was a hint of sarcasm in her voice.

He snatched the knob and jerked it open. "I'm sure," he said. "Now, what're you doin' down here? What do you want?"

"I want to know if Chris had a will."

He didn't know what he'd expected her to say, but it definitely wasn't that. His brows drew down. "What the hell are you asking a thing like that for?"

"Because I want to know." Solemn blue eyes bored into his. "Did he?"

It was an accusation. He didn't need it spelled out. "You must've kept real busy in town this afternoon, listenin' to all the gossip."

"No one gossiped," Dori said flatly. "I told you I met Jake's teacher, Maggie Tanner. She just indicated some surprise when I said Jake had inherited Chris's half of the ranch. She understood there wasn't a will. *Was there?*"

Riley looked away. He jammed his hands into the pockets of his jeans. He rocked back on the heels of his boots. Then he rocked forward and came down on his toes, hard. "No, there wasn't." He said the words with as much force as she'd spoken hers, daring her to make something of it.

"Then Jake doesn't own half the ranch."

"Yes, he does."

"But if Chris didn't leave it to him, it's yours."

"It's Jake's," Riley insisted.

"Not if—"

"Did Chris send you money for Riley?"

"Yes. But that's not—"

"It was money from Chris's share of the ranch. Whatever profits Chris made, they went to Jake."

"But—"

"Don't you think if Chris had made a will, he'd have left the ranch to Jake?" he demanded.

The blue eyes blinked, looking suddenly confused. "I don't...I don't know. The point is, he didn't."

"The point is, he would have. And I knew it. Once I knew about Jake, I knew Chris's half belonged to him."

"But legally—"

"Legally it's Jake's. Chris's name is on his birth certificate. Chris is his father. Jake is Chris's heir."

"How do you know Chris is on his birth certificate?"

"Because I checked."

She stared at him.

"When they sent me Chris's effects and I found out about Jake in the first place, I knew Chris would want him to have it. My lawyer didn't believe in my giving up what he figured was mine by rights. So I had to prove to him that Jake was Chris's son."

"You didn't have to," she argued.

"Yes," Riley said flatly. "I did."

"Why?" Her voice almost trembled now. She shook her head as if she didn't understand. He didn't blame her.

But he wasn't sure he wanted her to understand, either. He shrugged. "Because it belongs to him," he said simply. "It's Jake's."

They stared at each other, she, searching his face, asking him questions he didn't want to answer; he, trying to stay steady, to get through this, to shut her up and hope she would go away.

"You were going to *buy* it from him. Pay him money for

something that you could have had without spending a dime."
She said the words in an almost dreamy tone, as if she was
trying to figure them out as she spoke.

"Then it would have been mine," Riley agreed. "The right
way."

"That's what you wanted." She swallowed. Her words were
soft. She didn't look at him now, but instead stared out the
doorway into the growing darkness.

"Yeah." He shifted from foot to foot. "It's what I'd
planned."

She didn't reply for a moment. Then she gave an almost
harsh, broken laugh. "Boy, we really must have made your
day when we showed up and moved in."

Riley's mouth twisted. "It was a shock," he admitted.

"Why didn't you say? Why didn't you just tell us to go
away?"

"I couldn't." That was the simple truth. He shrugged. "You
weren't going to kill Jake's dreams."

She gave him a wry look. "So I killed yours instead."

"No." He hesitated. "Mine were already dead."

In the instant after he said the words, he regretted it. He
didn't talk about his dreams ever, not to anybody.

Dori opened her mouth as if to ask him a question, then
apparently saw the look on his face and thought better of it.
"I'm sorry."

"Not your fault."

"A whole lot of everything else is my fault."

"No. It…it hasn't been bad. Jake's…Jake's fun." He smiled
a little. "A good kid. A good hand. I've…enjoyed him." He
rocked back and forth on his boot heels again, watching his
toes, slanting a quick glance her way.

"Then it's just me you don't like?"

His head jerked up. *"What?"*

"You don't look at me. You rarely talk to me—except to
tell me not to wash your clothes or bake cookies or do what I
can to help. You walk out of rooms that I come in. You won't
sit down in the evening and watch a program with Jake because
I'm there, too. You don't like me." She folded her arms across

her chest and stared at him, as if daring him to dispute her interpretation of the facts.

"I like you! And I do, too, look at you!" His face was warm now from doing that very thing. Every time he looked at her, his face seemed to get hot. "And I talk to you. I've just been talkin' to you, haven't I? And it isn't necessary for you to *do* things for me all the time—"

"Like wash your shirts."

It wasn't the *shirts* that bothered him. He rubbed a hand against the back of his neck. "I don't want to take advantage," he muttered.

"I think the 'taking advantage' bit has been all mine," Dori said dryly. "I think Jake and I don't belong here. I think I should sign the contract on his behalf and take a pittance, if you won't just take the ranch back for nothing, and then I think Jake and I should get out of your way."

"No! I don't—I don't want him—you—to go!" He took a deep breath and tried to put his thoughts in order, to say them to her so they'd make sense. "That's what I wanted in the beginning—to buy the ranch, to have it all for myself, once and for all, fair and square. It would have been tight financially, but I would have managed. I intended to manage—because that's what Chris would have wanted—and because it's the right thing to do, and I wanted to do it, too.

"But when you...when you came...with Jake—" The words got a little harder now. It wasn't quite so easy to explain how his feelings had changed since they'd been here. All he could say was, "It's better this way."

She looked doubtful.

"It is." He looked at her, straight at her. "I want you to stay."

"You want *Jake* to stay."

"Both of you," he said. He didn't know if he meant that or not. Dori caused him no end of confusion. He wanted her there. He wanted her gone. But he knew for a fact that if she went, so would Jake.

Apparently his lack of conviction showed. She looked equally unconvinced.

"Where would you go?" he challenged her after a moment. She gave a bitter smile. "Not home, that's for sure."

"Would you really take Jake away? He's happy here."

"I know that. I just…feel 'beholden.'" Her expression told him how little she liked the feeling.

"You're not. It's not necessary."

Her blue eyes flashed. "If you say that one more time, I'll leave right now! It is necessary for me to do my part. I'll tell you what," she said, "we'll stay—for now—if you let me contribute—if you don't refuse my cookies and my washing and folding clothes. If you let me work around here and supplement the income by working, too."

*She would stay if he let her wash his shorts?* Riley closed his eyes. And what the hell was this nonsense about working? "What do you mean working?"

"I know how to do bookkeeping. You've got a computer. If I get the right software I can maybe get some work keeping books and inventories for a few of the businesses in town. If you'll 'let me.'" Her chin challenged him again, and she gave the last two words a definite twist.

He stared at her. A good twenty seconds must have passed. Then, "You know computers?" he asked.

She nodded.

"You do…book work?" He sounded like a drowning man who'd just seen a life preserver bob into view.

"I learned from Milly, my sister. She got her degree in accounting at Montana State. She did the books for the store for years. But she taught me when she thought she was moving to Denver."

Riley didn't care where she'd learned. He only cared that she knew how.

"You'll stay if I let you do book work?" He almost laughed.

And something sparkled in Dori's eyes. It was almost as if she were laughing inside, too. "And the laundry."

He gave her a look of long-suffering despair. She looked back with perfect equanimity. Finally he muttered, "You drive a hard bargain."

She smiled then. It lit her whole face. "I do, don't I?" Then she held out her hand to him.

He stared at it. He hadn't touched Dori Malone yet. He wasn't sure he wanted to. It seemed even a little more intimate than her involvement with his underwear. But he also didn't see that he had a choice. If he didn't, she'd start thinking he didn't *like* her again. Cripes. He took her hand in his.

He hadn't held a girl's hand since Tricia's.

*Oh, for God's sake, why did he have to start thinking about that?*

Dori figured right off that she had to begin as she meant to go on.

If she just sort of easily stepped up the pace of her contribution to the ranch, Riley would think that was all there was—and whenever she tried to take it to the next level, they'd fight about it again.

So she took down all the curtains, washed all the windows, bought several gallons of paint, drove down to Casper and bought wood to replace the splintered railings around the porch, and started sewing, painting, sawing and hammering with a vengeance.

It wouldn't have been her choice to have four or five projects going at once. But she could do what she had to.

And one look at Riley's face when he saw the extent of her determination made her glad she had.

"What the hell are you doing?" he demanded when he came into the kitchen that first night to find evening light pouring through all the bare windows.

"Cleaning house," she said. "Making curtains. Painting rooms. Fixing the porch rail. Doing my part," she finished firmly, meeting his gaze straight-on, daring him to tell her it wasn't necessary.

He opened his mouth, then closed it again. He sighed. He scowled.

She smiled. Brightly. "After you've cleaned up for supper, bring me your laundry."

"I don't—"

"Or I'll go down to the bunkhouse and get it."

She would, too. She'd had enough of his stubbornness. She could be just as stubborn. She was, after all, John Malone's daughter.

After supper he brought up his laundry. He put it in the washing machine himself, though. Not giving her a chance to do it. But then he got distracted when Jake asked him about something to do with one of the horses. He never did come back to put it in the dryer or to fold it.

Dori moved to the dryer. And when it was done, she smoothed and folded it herself.

She hadn't given it much thought before. She'd washed enough laundry in her life to do it automatically. But since Riley had made such a big deal out of it, she found herself very aware of the soft cotton of the shirts and T-shirts that stretched across his broad back and the soft jeans that were almost white where he balanced bales of hay against his thighs and along the inseam where his legs rubbed on his saddle.

Mostly, though, she found herself lingering over his briefs.

There was nothing very special about them. They were white. They were cotton. They had been totally unmemorable.

Until she'd seen him in them the other evening.

She couldn't get the memory out of her mind.

Her fingers played with the elastic of the waistband. They traced the opening of the fly. They seemed to somehow, of their own volition, make a fist right there and—

Dori let out a whoosh of a breath. *Stop that! Just stop it!*

It was bad enough that she watched him all the time, that she seemed aware of his every movement, while he seemed oblivious to hers. Now she was developing a fetish about his underwear, too!

Maybe she ought to let him wash his own clothes.

No. She couldn't. Not after she'd made such a fuss about it.

She shoved the thought from her mind, finished folding the laundry, while deliberately focusing her mind on the painting she was going to begin on tomorrow in Jake's bedroom. A much safer topic.

Except she started thinking that it had once been Riley's bedroom, too.

Every morning when she went in there to make sure Jake had straightened his bed and left things in fairly reasonable order, she found herself staring at the pictures on the wall. At first she'd looked at the photos of the young Chris.

It had been interesting to see him as a boy. There was a free-spiritedness about him even then—a kind of devil-may-care attitude that came through even in print. Everyone else in the photo might be serious, but Chris was always larking about. The pictures confirmed everything she'd ever known about the man who was the father of her son.

She found herself going back, though, not to look again at Chris, but to look at Riley.

There was never anything devil-may-care about Riley Stratton. Not from the earliest school pictures, to the one of him and his father and a very big fish, to one of Riley sporting a big gold rodeo buckle, to a posed portrait of him with his arm around a pretty little blonde.

Dori wondered what had happened to the blonde.

Was she part of those dreams he said had died?

She didn't think it was something she ought to ask.

Jake could ask Riley a million questions, and he'd take the time to answer all of them. Dori could ask him if he wanted another cup of coffee or seconds on pork chops, and that was that.

She got Jake's bedroom painted. She got the curtains made. She would have liked to paint the bedroom she was sleeping in, but since it was Riley's really, she didn't think she should without asking him.

So one night later that week at dinner she said, "Do you mind if I paint your bedroom?"

"You want to paint the bunkhouse now?" He looked up at her, startled.

"Not the bunkhouse. Your bedroom. The one I'm sleeping in."

"Oh." He looked momentarily confused, then shrugged.

"It's your bedroom now. And you seem to get a charge out of painting, so do what you want."

There was encouragement for you, Dori thought.

"And then I'll be down to paint the bunkhouse," she informed him. "No big deal. I'll use the paint I have left over."

He gave her a baleful look, but didn't protest, though she knew he would have liked to.

"I thought I'd paint it pink."

Riley choked. "The hell you—"

Dori laughed. "Gotcha."

She had him, all right.

Everywhere he turned, there she was. Fixing the porch rail. Painting the bedrooms. Making curtains. *Doing his laundry.*

Every time he put on his shorts now, he thought about her fingers having been there before him.

He was going nuts.

It was like high school all over again. Like all those months that Tricia had teased him and tempted him and let him go home aching.

But she'd done it on purpose.

Dori Malone wasn't. She teased him, yeah. But not the way Tricia had—not with soft kisses and playful nibbles, not with the brush of her breasts against his arm or the exploration of roving hands.

Dori's idea of teasing was telling him she was going to paint his bunkhouse pink or asking if maybe he'd like to take her along when he moved the cattle up to the summer pasture. He knew she could get a rise out of him. It was entirely verbal.

She never touched him at all.

He only wished.

It wasn't her, he told himself. Not her specifically, that is. It was him.

He was a healthy normal male with all the right instincts—instincts he'd kept reined in for years and years. Instincts he might have managed to keep well reined in forever if Jake's very pretty mother hadn't appeared.

But she had. And she enticed him merely by being there—

by cooking and baking and painting and sewing, by smelling good and doing laundry and smiling at him over dinner at the end of every day.

She and Jake together reminded him of everything he'd once dreamed of. She, in particular, made him think about all the things he was missing. And wanted.

Still wanted.

*Bad.*

Dori had what she wanted.

She was contributing. The rooms all had new curtains. Both bedrooms and the alcove were painted—blue, not pink. She had scrubbed and polished and waxed the floors. Her mother would have been proud—if she didn't drop dead from shock first.

Dori had never been a committed housekeeper. All those womanly tasks that she was excelling at now were not the things she would have chosen to do.

She would have chosen to saddle up and ride out with Riley and Jake.

But she knew even a hint of that would have been pushing too hard.

And it wasn't as if she could have contributed much if she had saddled up. Despite her dreams and her childhood fantasies, she knew darn well she'd have been more of a liability on horseback than she would have been a help.

So she was stuck in the house. For the moment, at least.

She did take over the computer, though. For all the times Riley occasionally disappeared into the alcove under the pretense of "working," mostly what she glimpsed him doing in there was reading the instruction manuals and scowling at the screen. That was when she discovered that he wore glasses.

They made him look almost as sexy as he did in just his briefs—a thought that she didn't dare pursue. She spent enough time daydreaming about Riley Stratton in various forms of dress and undress.

She needed now to think of him as her partner—*Jake's* partner. And nothing else.

So she'd hoped he would invite her into the alcove with him. She'd hoped he would say, "Come help me with this." When they'd struck their "bargain," he had, after all, seemed interested in her doing the book work.

But she waited. And waited. And the words never passed his lips. Pretty soon she realized that unless she pushed, he wouldn't "think it was necessary," and she'd wait forever before he ever brought it up again.

So the next time he went into the bedroom to turn on the computer, she waited until he was sitting at the keyboard and then she followed him in.

"So," she said, coming up behind him and deliberately sounding as brisk and businesslike as she could, "show me what needs to be done."

He almost jumped a foot. He shot up out of the chair and spun around to glare at her. "Who invited you in?"

"You did," she said, refusing to retreat an inch. "You gave me your bedroom, remember?" she said, gesturing behind her toward the bed where she slept every night. "And you did say something about book work when we talked."

"It's not nec—" He stopped. He scowled. They both knew what he'd intended to say.

Finally Riley rubbed his hands over his hair and let out a harsh exhalation of air. "I hate this stuff," he admitted.

"Let me see." Dori fetched a chair from the kitchen and came to sit next to him. He moved to make room for her. She could tell he was trying to give her *a lot* of room. But the space was limited. They were wedged in there together.

It was, she realized, perhaps not the brightest move she'd ever made. Not if she wanted to keep her mind on the computer program, at least.

*Which you do,* she reminded herself.

So she tried to pay attention to what he told her. She tried not to notice that sometimes when he moved the mouse, their elbows bumped and if he shifted—or she did—their thighs brushed. She tried not to wonder exactly why he cleared his throat a lot and seemed to lose track of what he was saying halfway through each sentence.

Finally he shoved back his chair in disgust. "This isn't working!"

"Let me just look at it for a while by myself, okay? You go see Jake or do whatever else you want to do, and when I need you, I'll come looking."

The minute she said the words, she realized they hadn't come out exactly the way she'd intended. Her cheeks burned. She gave herself a quick shake. She wet her lips and stole one quick glance in Riley's direction.

"About the book work, I mean," she clarified.

"Of course," Riley said. His voice was oddly hoarse. "Go to it," he muttered, and left without looking back.

It was better when he wasn't there. Well, not *better* precisely. But she could pay attention now. She started reading the fields across the top of the database. "Cows. Calves. Sex." No, it didn't mean *that!* "Birth weight. Vaccinations."

Focus. Concentrate. Understand.

She didn't think about his nearness anymore. She didn't tingle with awareness at the merest brush of his shirtsleeve against hers. She could do this. Yes, she could.

The phone rang.

She picked it up, expecting it to be for Riley, who never answered it even when he was in the house. Surprisingly, a woman asked for her.

"It's Maggie," the woman said when Dori identified herself. "I'm calling to see if you and Riley and Jake can come out to our place for a barbecue a week from Saturday. I'd try to do it sooner, but Robert has to go to Denver for a few days. And then his brothers are coming and we're having a little reunion, so we thought maybe we'd have you all come, too, and a few neighbors and friends."

"I— That sounds…great," Dori said. "I'll have to ask Riley, of course."

"Don't *ask* Riley. Just tell him. If you give him a choice, he'll always have work to do so that he can't come."

"You know him pretty well." In the time they had been here, Riley hadn't stopped yet.

"It's not just Riley, it's the breed," Maggie said cheerfully.

"Robert's the same way. We've been married nine years now, and I'm still trying to reform him."

"I'm looking forward to meeting him," Dori said. "To meeting all of them."

"And they'll be looking forward to you, too, believe me," Maggie said. There was a great deal of pleasure in her voice. "And the boys are really eager to meet Jake. See you then."

"Yes," Dori said. She sat holding the receiver in her hand long after Maggie had hung up.

*Don't ask Riley. Tell him.*

No, she wasn't quite brave enough to do that.


He wished to hell Maggie Tanner would mind her own business.

At least, he wished that one second. The next Riley knew he ought to be glad she was taking the initiative to introduce Jake—and Dori—to the community.

Probably he should have done it himself—had a shindig and invited everybody out here to meet them.

Except Riley had the social graces of a Trappist. He'd never entertained anyone in his life.

So Maggie was going to do it for him.

She'd called Dori and invited them. Dori had told him last night. And Dori had said yes.

Of course Dori had said yes.

Why wouldn't she? She probably *wanted* to go and be the center of attention and meet all the local ranchers and townspeople and have Jake meet Maggie and Tanner's boys and make friends with the other kids his age.

Trouble was, Riley didn't want to.

It wasn't that he was antisocial. He liked a party as well as the next guy. He just liked being on the sidelines of a party. He didn't like being the focus. And while he knew Maggie was ostensibly having them over for everybody to meet Dori and Jake, he also knew his neighbors well enough to know that they'd be looking at him, too. Looking—and conjecturing.

"Ol' Riley's got a gal at his place," Ev Warren or another

one of the grizzled old cowhands would say, a wealth of speculation and more than a hint of envy in his tone.

And it wasn't just the men who'd be thinking, either.

The women would be doing some calculating, too. Maggie. Sam Gallagher's wife, Sue. Rick Walker's wife, Tracy. Lucy Haverford at the post office, a busybody if there ever was one. Gretchen, who waited tables at Champion's, and Sybil, the checker at the hardware store. Not to mention Suellen Flynn, the doc's wife.

And Tricia.

Riley didn't doubt for a minute that Tricia and Jeff would be there. Certainly they would. Jeff would want to meet this nephew that Riley had given half the ranch to. And Tricia would, too.

Jeff wouldn't have told her about Jake, Riley knew that. The lawyer was an absolute stickler about client confidentiality, Riley had to give him that.

But even if Jeff never said a word, it wouldn't have taken long for word to pass through the community. Dori had come through town on the way to the ranch. Dori had gone back into town and met teachers, shopkeepers and God knew who all.

If one knew—they all knew.

So Tricia knew.

He wondered what Tricia would think of Jake.

He wondered what she'd think of Dori.

# Seven

"Ya know," Jake said to his uncle as they saddled up their horses early the next morning, "someday we oughta bring Mom along."

Uncle Riley tightened his cinch strap and grunted a reply. Jake wasn't sure if it was a yes or a no. Uncle Riley didn't usually have much to say early in the morning. Probably, Jake thought, he should have waited and brought it up later.

"She's a pretty good rider," he added. After all, he'd started now. He couldn't really drop it and then start up again in an hour or two. He'd been thinking about his mom not getting to be a cowboy for a while now.

At first he'd been too busy to think about it. He'd been so excited that *he* was getting to be a cowboy, that he hadn't thought about anybody else. And he'd been pretty tired, too. Most nights when he and Uncle Riley got home, it was all he could do to keep his eyes open during dinner. Sometimes he watched TV or read a book after. But pretty often he just went to bed.

Being a cowboy was everything Jake had hoped it would be. But he wasn't sure it was so great for his mother.

As far as he could see, she didn't get to do any fun stuff at all.

"Why don'tcha come with us sometime?" he'd asked her last night when she was tucking him in. He'd been a little more awake than usual, and she'd told him a story. The "stardust cowboy" story, because he'd insisted. "'Cause it's real now," he'd told her.

And so she'd told him the story, using stuff that he described about the things he did with Uncle Riley all day.

And that was when he realized that he knew more about cowboying now than she did.

"Maybe the stardust cowboy should take you on an adventure," he'd suggested when she'd finished telling him the story and was bending down to kiss him good-night.

"Oh, I think you're having adventures enough for both of us," she said, ruffling his hair. And she'd smiled as she'd kissed him.

But after she'd left, he'd lain there thinking about it. It wasn't fair that he should have all the fun. Besides, just because she came along didn't mean he wouldn't come, too. They could both go cowboying with Uncle Riley.

"We could bring her next time we move cattle," he said now as they headed out. "An' we could bring a picnic an' eat at the swimming hole. That'd be cool, wouldn't it?"

But Uncle Riley was riding a little ahead and when he didn't answer, Jake wasn't sure if he even heard.

He'd heard, all right.

He just didn't know what to say. Somehow he didn't think telling Jake that there was no way on God's earth he was going to bring his mother along would go over all that well.

But he wasn't.

He spent enough of his life aware of Dori Malone. He got to see her every morning when she was fixing them breakfast. He watched her every evening when he went up for dinner. If he could have confined her to the kitchen, it might have been all right. But sometimes he saw her sitting on the porch, drying her hair in the evening breeze, brushing it out and letting the light westerly wind billow it around her face. And sometimes he saw her sitting on the couch next to Jake, her arm around him, both their heads bent over a book. And sometimes he had to sit right next to her while she talked to him about the stuff she'd put into the computer. Then she would point at something and turn and look right at him—her eyes only inches from his, her mouth so close he could see the tiny nick in her front tooth. And sometimes when she talked, she gestured, and her fingers brushed his sleeve or her hand touched his thigh.

And if all that wasn't bad enough, sometimes she invaded his dreams.

Riley had never had such dreams.

None that he'd ever remembered, anyway.

These he couldn't seem to forget. And that made it damned difficult to look her in the face!

So when Jake said they ought to bring his mother along during the day, Riley's instant reaction was *No!*

His day's work was the only respite he had. He didn't need Dori Malone invading that as well.

But Jake, once he latched on to a notion, didn't give it up easily. Riley had hoped that ignoring him in the morning would put an end to the topic. But they happened to be making a circle up near the swimming hole that afternoon.

"Mom would love this," Jake said. "I say we bring her. She never gets to do anything fun."

"Well, then, maybe *you* should bring her," Riley said at last. They were sitting by the water's edge, having taken a swim already. They ought to be moving on. There was some fence down south Riley needed to check. But it was warm in the sun, and the lunch Dori had packed them made him feel fat and lazy.

"We could *all* come," Jake suggested.

"I've got work to do." Riley picked up a rock and flipped it, then watched it skip four…five…six…seven times. He grinned, satisfied that he hadn't lost the knack. Then he turned his attention back to Jake. "But I think it's a great idea for you to do it with her. You can do it tomorrow while I'm up movin' cattle.''

"But I want you, too," Jake said. "Can'tcha come, Riley?"

"No."

"But—"

"No!"

If there was one thing he didn't need, it was to know what Dori Malone looked like in a swimming suit.

Now this was more like it.

Dori sat back in the saddle and lifted her face to the sun and breathed deeply of the sweet Wyoming air. It was possible, she thought, that coming with Jake today was going to be a mistake. It would give her an idea of what she was missing when she was home computing or cleaning or doing what needed to be done at the house.

But she couldn't say no when he'd suggested it last night at dinner. "Uncle Riley says he's got to go to the high pasture tomorrow, and so I wondered if you'd want to come ride fence with me."

She had arched her brows and looked at Riley, curious about how he thought she and a seven-year-old were going to be able to ride fence, especially since she didn't know what she was doing.

Riley had just shrugged. "Don't worry. You'll be fine."

Dori thought he was probably right. She'd learned to trust his judgment about ranch matters over the past few weeks. And she'd learned to trust the way he handled Jake. He gave Jake responsibility, but never more than the boy could handle. It was impressive the way he'd developed Jake's sense of competence. She sometimes thought he was a better father than Chris would have been.

*That surprises you?* she asked herself. *How could it, when Riley is here and Chris never even wanted to be around?*

Well, it didn't surprise her. But it did make her just the tiniest bit wistful. Here he was, great dad material—not to mention, lean, dark, handsome and just a little shy—and he wasn't married. It was a waste, she thought.

"Why don't you marry Uncle Riley?" Jake's voice, saying words she never dared even think, broke into her thoughts.

*"What?"* She turned and stared at her son, aware that her face was flaming, hoping that if Jake noticed, he would put it down to the effects of the sun. *"What did you say?"*

Jake had the grace to look slightly abashed. "I was just thinkin' that we're already sort of a family. An' most families are moms and dads and kids. An' you get along. An' sometimes he looks at you…you know…kinda…interested—" Now it was Jake's turn to color. "I just thought it was a good idea."

"Well, stop thinking," Dori said sharply. "And stop matchmaking."

"What's matchmaking?"

"Trying to find a husband for your mom."

"I don't have to find one. There's one already here," Jake said. "Uncle Riley."

"Your uncle Riley doesn't want to get married."

"How do you know?"

"He told me. He said he wasn't ever getting married. That's why he said you'd be the heir to the ranch."

"That's stupid."

Dori actually shared that opinion, but she didn't think telling Jake so was a very good idea. "It's what he said."

Jake looked disgusted. "Well, maybe I can change his mind."

*"Don't you dare! Don't you say one word to him!"* Heavens, that was all she needed to make things even more awkward between herself and Chris's brother.

Jake didn't say anything, just touched his heels to the sides of his horse and led the way up the slope. Dori wanted a promise from him, but she couldn't yell at him. So she followed, determined to get it when they stopped again.

But she forgot about it when they came to the crest of the hill and she looked down on the most beautiful little river. The view contained everything she thought Western scenery ought to have. The grassy slope on which their horses stood led gently down to the curve of the river. The river itself was lined with cottonwoods. A half-dozen cattle stood chewing grass; four more lounged in the shade of the trees. It was all very bucolic and peaceful. Beyond them, through the trees, she saw the sparkle of still more water.

"What's that ?" she pointed.

"The swimmin' hole I been tellin' you about. C'mon." Jake urged his horse into a trot, and once more Dori followed.

The swimming hole was a treat. Jake, of course, leaped off his horse, loosened the cinch, stripped down to his briefs and jumped in. "Aren'tcha comin' in, Mom?" he yelled from the middle, teeth chattering.

He'd told her to wear her swimsuit. "You gotta swim," he'd urged.

She'd looked to Riley for guidance then, too, but he hadn't allowed himself to be dragged into that. He'd kept his nose very firmly in the local paper and he hadn't looked up once.

So Dori had allowed herself to be coerced into donning her suit beneath her jeans. "What about you?" she'd asked her son when they'd left that morning. "Do you have yours on?"

"Nope. Uncle Riley says that's what undershorts are for."

Was that what Uncle Riley wore when they swam? Undoubtedly. Dori had a vision of Riley in his shorts, dripping wet. So much for her peace of mind.

She stripped off her own clothes down to her bathing suit and plunged into the water. It was shockingly cold.

Good, she thought. The better to banish her heated thoughts.

They swam for half an hour. Then they got out and sat on the sandstone rock near the bank and ate the lunch she had brought.

"Do you and...Uncle Riley...come up here often?" she asked.

Jake finished chewing before he answered. "Not as often as I want to," he said. "But we come fairly often. There's cattle up this way we got to check. I should check on those." He jerked his head toward the bunch munching their way through the pasture across the river.

"You know what to look for?" Dori asked him.

"Pinkeye. And any cuts or stuff like that. And they gotta look bright. Not sicklike, you know?"

Dori wasn't sure, but apparently Jake had an idea.

"I'm learnin'," he told her.

Yes, he was.

It had been a good thing, their move to the ranch. Jake had been doing all right back in Livingston, but he was thriving here. Thanks to Riley Stratton's generosity, his dreams were coming true.

Now she looked over at him as he stretched out on the rocks. He was lean and brown and wiry. But there were more muscles in his arms. He was lither, stronger. He moved with a quick grace now that reminded her of his uncle more than of his father. It was good they had come.

It was.

And if she sometimes wished for more, she knew she had no right.

She'd come for Jake's dreams, not for her own.

It was just her bad luck that she couldn't stop thinking about Riley.

It was at dinnertime, when they were all back home, and she was watching Riley not watching her that she remembered what Jake had said.

"He's, um…interested in you," he'd told her that afternoon.

What did a not-quite-eight-year-old boy know about men being interested in women? she wondered.

But the more she tried to catch Riley's eye that evening, the more she wondered if perhaps Jake could be right. When he was telling Riley about the swimming hole and about them lying out in the sun on the rocks after, then Riley had sneaked a quick look at her. Was he wondering what she'd looked like in her swimsuit?

Oh, Dori, you dreamer, she chided herself.

Well, she'd wondered what he would look like in his briefs. *She* was interested—for all the good it seemed to be doing her.

He was, damn it, very good-looking. He didn't seem aware

of it, though. Chris had always known his power over women. Riley was oblivious.

But was he oblivious to her?

*Dori, don't!*

But she couldn't help it. She'd spent the entire time she'd been at the ranch aware of him—*very* aware of him. And Jake said he was "interested" in her. Was it possible?

She owed it to both of them, she decided, to do a little experiment.

"I want to show you something," she said to Riley as she was clearing the table. "After I'm finished here—if you don't mind hanging around."

He looked surprised, then a little confused. But he said, "Er, no. Sure. I'll wait." But then he shrugged and went off with Jake to the corral. He and Jake were working with a young paint that Riley thought would make a good mount for Jake down the road.

"He's young yet. Needs the kinks worked out. We'll see. We'll take it slow and see how it goes," he'd said when he'd proposed they work with this new horse.

It had sounded good to Dori when he proposed it. So far it seemed to be going well. And as a method of operation, it wasn't that far different from what she was planning tonight.

She and Riley would just "take it slow and see how it went."

She booted up the computer and started the program she'd been using the past few days. She'd been entering the mamma cows and recording the bulls who'd been the daddies, and the estimated birth weights of their offspring. She really did have something to show him. And if she had an ulterior motive, well…she had an ulterior motive.

"So, shoot me," she muttered.

Then she brushed her hair, took a quick shower and put on clean clothes. It was when she was reaching for her bra that she hesitated. She stood there, holding it against her breasts, considering. Her breasts were her one asset. They had always been something of a drawing card where men were concerned.

Where *Riley* was concerned?

A small smile played on her lips. Maybe it wouldn't hurt to find out.

She debated spraying just a hint of cologne on, then decided he would definitely "get wind that something was up" if she did that. She considered applying a little blush, too, but a look in the mirror told her it wasn't necessary. Nature had provided plenty of that.

Then, drawing a deep breath, she opened the door and went out, heading toward the corral where he and Jake were working with the young paint gelding.

When he saw her coming, he left Jake and ambled toward her with a look of curiosity on his handsome face.

Handsome, in fact, didn't begin to cover it. He was gorgeous. In a rugged, intensely masculine way, Riley Stratton had all the most appealing adjectives covered. He should have been in one of those commercials with rough-hewn cowboys doing what they did best.

The very thought brought the blush even more intensely to Dori's cheeks. "Cool it," she muttered to herself, rubbing her suddenly damp palms against the sides of her jeans.

Getting close to Riley was like getting close to a wild animal. He was wary and innocent at the same time.

And she was very likely an idiot to be doing this.

But, idiot or not, she wanted to know....

She *had* to know if something could come of it...if she would be allowed her dreams, too.

Because she realized then—or maybe she'd realized for a while, but only managed to articulate then—that Riley was the man of her dreams.

As a young woman, she'd thought it was Chris. At least, Chris had come the closest to embodying what she thought she wanted in a man. He was a man of the land, a man of vision, of determination, of dreams.

But his dreams were different from her own.

Then she'd thought they could mesh them, could overcome the differences, could become not just lovers for a time, but a man and woman who would go through life together.

She'd seen in Portland how wrong she'd been. She'd seen

then how she'd endowed Chris with attributes he not only didn't have, but didn't want. Whether she wanted it or not, she knew then that they were destined to go through life as partners in having given Jake life, and that was all.

Their paths had converged for a time, and then had gone in very different directions.

But Chris's path had brought her here.

He had brought her to his ranch, to his brother—to a man much closer to her dream man. To a man who might—or might not—be "interested" in her.

And if he was?

No. First she had to find out. Then…then…

Then they would "see."

She just prayed she hadn't fallen in love once more with the wrong man.

Riley had spent the day trying not to think about Dori in a bathing suit.

It was like trying to spend a day telling yourself not to think about elephants. Harder in fact. Riley's mind did not naturally gravitate toward elephants. It seemed to make a beeline for Dori Malone every time he wasn't determinedly directing it somewhere else.

"You could have gone with 'em," he reminded himself over and over.

*Oh, yeah, what a great idea that would have been,* a small sarcastic inner voice commented.

Fortunately he had a little more willpower than that. And a little more common sense. She was his nephew's *mother,* for crying out loud! The woman who had loved his brother. She was a guest in his house.

"She *lives* in your house, you idiot," he muttered to himself.

Exactly. All the more reason to steer clear of her.

Which was precisely what he had been doing. What he would continue to do—just as soon as she showed him whatever marvel she intended to show him on the computer.

He had to admit she made sense of the computer. All his computer problems had been solved since Dori had taken over.

Now she intended to do "queries," she'd told him. "Look for significant trends. See what the data can tell us."

It always told him he was in way over his head.

"Riley!"

He had been putting Jake and the young paint through their paces, but he turned when he heard her call. She was coming toward them, the light wind lifting and teasing her dark hair, tangling it. And when she reached them, his hand suddenly took on a life of its own and reached out to brush a strand of hair away from her cheek.

"You should tie it down when it's windy like this," he told her gruffly, annoyed with her for letting it blow loose and tempt him.

Instead of gathering it back and fishing a rubber band out of her pocket, where he knew damned well she always kept a couple, she shook her head, making her hair billow all the more. "Sometimes I get a headache if I do," she said.

Riley grunted, then jammed his hands into his pockets. "Do what you want."

She gave him one of her glorious smiles. "I will, thank you."

She actually sounded as if his permission, grudging as it was, meant something to her. He scowled. "So, what did you want to show me on the computer?"

"If you're ready now, come on. I've been tracking the birth weights of the calves for the past five years."

That sounded useful, at least. Riley told Jake to get down and take the saddle off the paint and walk him to cool him down. Then he followed Dori up to the house.

She hadn't waited, and she was probably a good ten paces ahead of him. It gave him ample opportunity to study the curve of her backside as he walked behind her. Why the hell couldn't women just walk? Why did they have to *sway* so damn much? She wasn't on board a ship, for heaven's sake!

"I brought a chair in from the kitchen so we could both sit down," she told him, glancing his way as she led him through the bedroom toward the little alcove office.

On his way past, he noticed that her damned filmy night-gown was lying up near the pillows of the bed. *His* bed!

He averted her gaze—and saw her swimsuit drying on a towel in front of the open window.

He shut his eyes.

And stumbled over the corner of the rug.

"Damn!" He caught himself just as she turned and caught his arm. They stood there, staring at each other. Riley's chest seemed to be heaving, as if he'd run a mile. Dori's, interestingly, did, too. And it seemed very…available…somehow.

He coughed and jerked back. "'M all right. Just clumsy. Bull in a china shop, y'know?"

Dori didn't say anything. She just smiled again. Then she went and sat down at the computer and patted the chair next to her, indicating that he should sit there.

Riley sat. He shifted. He fidgeted. He tried to get a little more room in his jeans. Inconspicuously, of course.

"Here's what I've done," Dori began.

He tried to pay attention. Really, he did. She showed him a list of all the mamma cows in the herd, then a list of each cow's calves and their birth weights. Then she brought up a screen that showed which bulls had impregnated which cows and the weights of the calves that had resulted. It was all very logical, Riley was sure.

Well, he would have been sure, if he hadn't been distracted.

But how the hell could he not be distracted when she was sitting inches from him, raising her arm to point out this field and that weight, and he kept noticing how she, well, *bobbed* when she did so.

And suddenly he realized why. She wasn't wearing a bra.

He almost said the words out loud. Then he almost gasped for air realizing what her reaction would have been if he had! Cripes!

"It is pretty amazing, isn't it?" Dori said.

"*What?*" He stared at her, dumbstruck.

"It's so obvious when you just look," she went on blithely.

His jaw must be dragging on the ground.

"Clear as anything, this bull is not doing the job." Her arm came up again and she stabbed a finger at the screen. Her breasts jiggled.

Riley swallowed.

"So then I began to think," she said. And damned if she didn't start comparing the relative virility of the bulls.

His mind reeled. His body had other things to do.

"He wasn't one of our bulls," she said, "and I was curious if other ranchers had recognized the same thing, so I called Robert Tanner and—"

"You did *what?*"

She'd talked to Tanner about…about *that?*

She looked worried. "Is that a breach of rancher etiquette?"

Riley shut his eyes. He prayed for strength, for fortitude, for the earth to open up and swallow him whole. Any—hell, *all* of the above!

"Riley? Did I…do something…wrong?"

He opened his eyes. Hers were scant inches away. When she blinked, he could almost count her individual lashes. He could count her freckles. He could kiss her mouth.

No! No, he couldn't do that. Not if he wanted to preserve his sanity.

"Did I, Riley?" she persisted. She wetted her lips.

Riley began to think that sanity was highly overrated. He shook his head.

"Riley?" Her brow furrowed. "Are you…all right?" She leaned closer.

*Wrong way, babe. Wrong way,* he wanted to tell her. Unfortunately he wasn't capable of words or, apparently, rational behavior.

His mouth did what his mind told him was a very bad thing indeed. It closed the space between them and touched hers.

And his mouth wasn't alone in its betrayal. His arms went around her, pulled her off her chair and onto his lap, needing to get her closer, to feel the warm weight of her body as well as the soft touch of her lips.

And he got it—he got it all. The warmth, the weight, the softness.

She seemed to want it as much as he did. Her hands traced

the line of his shoulders, then one cupped the back of his neck and the other played in his hair. And her lips—they moved, too, and opened under his. Her tongue touched his. A tremor ran through him as the heat of need, long denied, demanded release.

The kiss was long and sweet and reminded Riley of things he had been missing for years—like the sweet taste of a woman's lips beneath his, the soft press of her breasts against his chest, the way her bottom curved to fit neatly against the hardness of him. It was heady, intoxicating. It reminded him of the way he felt when he'd kissed Tricia.

*Tricia...*

The door banged, Jake's footsteps pounded down the hall. "Mom! Uncle Riley!"

Dori yanked herself back, off Riley's lap, out of his arms, onto her own chair. She shuddered and gulped air. Her face was blazing.

Riley reckoned his was, too.

"Mom!"

"In...here, dear," Dori's voice cracked a little. She cleared her throat. "I was just talking to Uncle Riley about...about a bull."

Jake skidded to a stop in the doorway. "Neat." He looked from one of them to the other, his eyes narrowing for a just a second. Then, whatever he thought, he seemed to recall what he'd come for. "Come look," he demanded. "I just saw a coyote!"

Yes, it would be coyote, Riley thought.

Coyote was the trickster. Befuddling men's minds. Shifting shape and bending reality.

Reality was that he was a hardened bachelor—in more ways than one—and she was a woman who had been way too long without a man.

He dragged in a harsh breath and looked at Dori.

He knew it was his turn to apologize. But he also knew that, mistake or not, just this one time he wasn't really sorry at all.

# Eight

They didn't see the coyote.

Riley wasn't surprised. Coyote was a tease, a tempter. He would have appreciated the discomfort Riley endured that night.

Coyote would have said it served him right for kissing a woman he had no business kissing. Or he would have, if coyote was given to righteousness. Riley wasn't sure about that.

He was sure he'd made a damned fool of himself where Dori was concerned.

Even if he wasn't sorry about the kiss, he was sorry that it was going to complicate their lives.

Now she'd think he was going to jump her bones every time he looked her way. She'd think he would try to take advantage of her. She'd think he *wanted* her!

Well, he did. But only physically. Only because she was there.

He didn't love her.

He was like his father, a one-woman man.

And that woman was Tricia.

* * *

He stayed away from Dori as much as he could for the rest of the week. He didn't want her to get the wrong idea.

He didn't want to take advantage.

Much.

But he couldn't help lying awake at night remembering the taste of her lips, the warmth of her body, the fullness of her breasts. He didn't get much sleep thinking about them. Thinking about *her*.

She had been Chris's lover. He told himself that over and over. She had doubtless reacted that way with Chris, too. Maybe she was like that with *all* the guys. It wouldn't surprise him.

Probably she would be all over the guys at the barbecue on Saturday.

He'd have to tell her it wasn't appropriate, tell her that Wyoming men didn't appreciate their women snuggling up to other women's husbands. Because that was who was going to be there—married men. Tanner and his brothers. Sam Gallagher. Both the Walkers. Mose from the welding shop. Jeff Cannon.

There might be one or two single fellows there, too, but she'd have to learn that it wasn't right to come on to them, either. It would be a reflection on Jake.

More, it would be a reflection on *him*.

Everybody would think he had brought a hussy into the neighborhood.

Yeah, he'd have to mention it to her.

But he couldn't seem to figure out when.


He was interested.

At least his body was. Dori wasn't as sure about his mind. Assuming that he had one. Men's minds had always been something of a mystery to her. Starting with her incomprehensible father, who seemed not to have anything other than ledger sheets and purchase orders on which to base his decisions, and moving on to her brother, Deke, whose responses were generally gut emotion, to Chris, who had been so bloody single-minded in pursuit of his dream, men had often seemed an alien—albeit occasionally intriguing—species.

Riley was more intriguing than most.

The kiss he'd given her intrigued the heck out of her. It was so...so...out of character. For as long as they'd been living here, he had appeared cool and practical and collected—a quiet, shy almost, but very competent cowboy. Determined to within an inch of his life. Honorable past that. But ultimately he'd seemed the epitome of balanced, measured, steady.

That kiss was anything but. It was not the kiss of a measured man. It spoke of passion and desire and deep, intense involvement. It was the sort of kiss one might associate with volcanic explosions.

But volcanoes didn't explode like that without a lot of internal seething having gone on underground first. It made her wonder just how long Riley had been smoldering.

And why.

She wished she dared ask.

But for all his passion, Riley was still quiet, still circumspect. Now—since the kiss—more than ever. He actually seemed to be avoiding her, watching her warily from afar, afraid to get close.

No, she couldn't ask Riley—and she didn't dare ask anyone else.

Perhaps she would hear something at the Tanners' barbecue. She was looking forward to that. She was counting on it being a way to get to know her neighbors and to find her place in the community. But she was also crossing her fingers that seeing Riley with these people who knew him so well would help her understand him.

She tried to get him to talk about them beforehand. "They'll be strangers," she'd said on Friday night. "I need you to help me know who's who."

Riley had scowled. "You'll get to know 'em soon enough," he replied, which didn't help at all. And then he added, "Just remember, most of the fellas are married."

Dori blinked. "Yes. And...?"

A flush crawled up his neck. "Just don't..." He rubbed a hand through his hair, then looked straight at her, blue eyes flashing. "Just don't!"

"Don't?"

But he'd turned his back and was striding toward the barn, leaving her to stare after him, trying yet again to fathom the mysterious workings of the male mind.

She didn't have a chance to bring up the issue again. He was gone all Saturday morning, moving some cattle to fresh pasture. Jake went with him as usual, bouncing and eager and full of questions about the Tanner boys.

Riley seemed not to have any reluctance when it came to discussing them.

Dori tried once again to figure out what he was thinking. But eventually she gave up and concentrated on baking a pan of brownies and making a couple of large bowls of potato salad to contribute to the food table.

She had checked with Maggie Tanner to see what "rancher etiquette" had to say about things like that. Maggie had been delighted with her offer to bring something.

"There's never enough, no matter how much I make," she'd said. "Bring whatever you like. Mostly just bring you and Jake. And Riley."

So Dori did.

They drove to the Tanner ranch, about fifteen miles south, late Saturday afternoon. They sat three abreast in Riley's truck, Jake in the middle, bouncing up and down, still asking questions.

Dori just sat, the big bowl of potato salad balanced on her lap, and listened to Jake's questions and Riley's answers, thinking all the while how very much they looked like a family.

It was like a dream come true. A dream that she'd put out of her mind for years and years. A dream she'd thought would never happen.

But here it was, almost within her grasp.

If Riley hadn't pursued her after the kiss they had shared, well, it was just that he was being circumspect. They could hardly have an affair with Jake in the house.

But they could, eventually, get married. There was nothing to stop them getting married. When Riley had said he wasn't ever getting married, it must have simply been because he'd never met the right woman.

But now...

Dori gave a little bounce on the seat, too, feeling almost as cheerful as Jake.


There were a lot of people at the Tanners' ranch. But almost at once Dori spied Maggie. She apparently spotted them, too, and came toward them, accompanied by a boy slightly taller than her twins.

She smiled as she greeted them. "Riley." She acknowledged him, then turned to Dori and Jake. "I'm so glad you could come. This is our oldest son, Jared. Jared," she said to the boy, "this is Jake. He's going to be in your class in school in the fall."

The two boys regarded each other solemnly for a moment. Then Jared said, "We got puppies. You wanta see 'em?"

Jake's eyes lit up. "You bet."

They ran off toward the house together. And that was all it took. Except Dori, well versed in the ways of sons, figured there might be a request for a puppy before the day was over.

She figured she would let Riley handle it. She glanced at him now. He had already made himself at home, leaning against the corral fence, a beer in his hand, talking to the dark-haired cowboy and another grizzled older one she remembered meeting outside the welding shop one afternoon.

"Ev," she said to herself, making sure she recalled his name. But Maggie overheard her. "Yes, that's Ev. You know Ev?"

"I met him in town one day."

"Ev's the one who keeps us going around here," Maggie said. "He keeps the boys out of trouble and Robert honest. Here, meet Sue Gallagher and give her the potato salad and give Tracy Walker the brownies, and I'll introduce you to everyone else."

Dori exchanged pleasantries with Sally and Tracy, two of the spouses of the "married men," relinquished the food to them and then followed Maggie to meet the rest.

"Sam Gallagher," Maggie said. "And Rick Walker, Tracy's

husband. And Jack Walker. His wife, Kathy, is the one pushing the little girl on the swing. They all ranch nearby.''

Dori smiled and said hello to them all. They were equally polite in return, touching the brims of their hats and nodding.

''That's your boy who went with Jared?'' Sam Gallagher asked her.

Dori nodded, feeling vaguely defensive, as if she might have to protect him from these people who would wonder about his coming in and usurping half of the Stratton ranch.

But Sam only nodded and smiled. ''He's got the look of a Stratton, all right.''

''He does,'' the Walker brothers agreed. They smiled at Dori, too.

She relaxed a little.

Maggie led her toward the corral fence where Riley and Ev and the dark-haired cowboy stood. ''You know Ev,'' she said to Dori, who smiled at the old man and shook his hand. ''And this is my husband, Robert.'' She introduced Dori to the handsome man she'd seen earlier catching a little girl jumping out of a tree house. ''You've talked to him on the phone. This is Dori,'' she said to her husband.

Robert Tanner took her hand in his rough, callused one and smiled at her, with a grown-up version of Jared's shy smile. His eyes twinkled. ''How's your bull?''

Out of the corner of her eye, Dori saw Riley choke and turn bright red. She knew she was coloring slightly, too. But she laughed and so did Robert Tanner.

Then he said, ''Glad to meet you finally. Can I get you a beer?''

He got her a beer. Maggie kept her moving, introducing more people.

''Dori, I'd like you to meet Robert's brothers. Luke, Noah, this is Dori Malone whose son, Jake, is Riley Stratton's nephew—and partner.''

A familiar voice said, ''Dori?''

And she found herself looking right into Noah Tanner's grinning face. ''Noah!''

Maggie looked from one to the other. "You two…have met?"

Dori was beaming, too. "Noah lives just north of where we used to live. In fact his partner, Taggart, is the one who let Jake come out and ride. Sometimes Susannah baby-sits—baby-sat—Jake."

"Which is more than she wants to do for us," Noah grumbled. Besides thirteen-year-old Susannah, he and Tess had two little boys, Clay, who was four, and Scott, who was two.

Now that she knew Clay and Scott were among them, she began to see the horde of little kids as individuals. In a moment she had picked both of Noah's boys out. She also saw Susannah sitting on a picnic bench talking to an earnest looking young blond cowboy.

So did her father. He frowned.

"That's just Billy," Maggie said, seeing, too, where her brother-in-law's gaze had gone. "Ev's grandson. Susannah will be fine."

"Which ones are yours?" Dori asked Luke.

He nodded toward the swing set where one little boy was swinging madly and far higher than all the rest. "That's Keith, the oldest. Katie—" he pointed to a little girl with long honey-colored hair pulled back in a ponytail who was trailing after Jared and Jake, who were carrying a puppy apiece "—and Jack is the one trying to decapitate his mother." His gaze turned toward a little boy who was hanging with his arms around the neck of a tall, slender woman. She held him absently while talking to the woman Dori recognized as Noah's wife.

"Maybe I'd better go rescue Jill," Luke said. He gave Dori a heart-stopping grin. She checked, just to be sure that with all these kids he also had the requisite wedding band. He did.

She sighed as she watched him walk away.

"He's a hunk, isn't he?" Maggie said.

"Mmm." Dori agreed. All the Tanner brothers were pretty impressive, as far as she was concerned. Of course, they didn't hold a candle to Riley Stratton, but…

She looked around to see where he was.

He was still by the corral, but he wasn't standing now. He

was hunkering down with Jake and Jared, looking over the puppies. As she watched, he took his hat off and scratched his head. His hair was exactly the same color as Jake's. He and Jake, heads together, looked as much alike as the Tanner boys and their fathers.

"Riley's very good with him, isn't he?" Maggie asked quietly.

"Mmm? Oh—" Dori felt a faint flush color her cheeks at having been caught watching "—yes, he is. Very."

"I'm so glad." Maggie said. "For both of them."

Dori would have liked to ask what she meant, but there were more people to meet. A rancher from east of the Interstate, Myron Thatcher, and his wife, Julie. Another teacher friend of Maggie's called Gayle Stevens. A doctor from Casper named Brent Walker. A lawyer named Jeff Cannon and his wife, Tricia.

Dori recognized the name *Cannon*. It had been on the top of the stationery on which Riley had offered to buy Jake's share of the ranch. And Jeff Cannon was looking at her very closely. She was pretty sure, given his demeanor, that Jeff Cannon was reserving judgment about how pleased he was to meet her. His wife, a pretty blonde, seemed curious, too.

"You're actually…living at Ri—er, Strattons'?" she asked Dori.

The censorious tone Dori had expected and hadn't received from the ranchers talking about Jake, seemed to creep into Tricia Cannon's voice now.

But Dori met it with a smile. "Yes, and it's wonderful there. We love it."

"It must be…tight quarters," Tricia said.

"Well, I do feel a little guilty about that," Dori replied. "But Riley says he doesn't mind living in the bunkhouse."

Tricia's eyes brightened. "He's in the bunkhouse?"

Her husband asked a few questions, too. Probing questions about Dori's background and where she met Chris and a few others that she would have thought extremely nosy and inappropriate, if she hadn't known the reason behind them. Jeff was Riley's lawyer. He was concerned and wanted to make sure that his client hadn't been taken advantage of.

Dori made it a point to answer his questions fully and with equanimity. She and Jake were going to live here a long time. It was—dared she hope?—possible that sometime Jeff might be *her* lawyer, too. She didn't want bad feelings.

So after Maggie excused herself to do something in the kitchen, Dori and Jeff talked. Tricia listened.

Dori thought Riley might come over and reassure his lawyer that she wasn't the wicked witch from Montana here to steal his land. But though he glanced their way from time to time, and Dori could tell from his expression that he was interested in what was going on, he made no move to intervene.

Eventually Jeff held out a hand again and she took it again, but this time there was a bit more of a hearty welcome in his grip. "I'm pleased to have met you at last," he said.

And Dori dared at least to hope that he was also pleased with her.

With the introduction to Jeff and Tricia Cannon, she seemed to have met everyone. "Come see those puppies," Maggie invited her, when she came back from the kitchen.

"You aren't by any chance looking for homes for them, are you?" Dori raised a suspicious eyebrow.

Maggie laughed. "Well, if you and Jake were to fall in love with one, I don't know if we could refuse you."

"Just what I was afraid of," Dori muttered.

"We won't force any on you. Don't worry," Maggie said.

"It isn't *you* I'm worried about."

But she allowed herself to be dragged over to meet the puppies Jake and Jared were holding. Riley held one, too, as did Susannah Tanner and a couple of the children Dori hadn't met yet. The pups were five-week-old border collies.

"Herding dogs," Robert Tanner said. "And good with kids," he added.

"Mmm," Dori said. But she let Jake thrust one into her hands. It was scarcely as big as a lunch box, but much wigglier and fluffier. It stuck out its tongue and licked her.

She laughed.

"Isn't he swell, Mom?" Jake said. His eyes were shining.

"He's…very nice," Dori said. He was darling, and she was

a sucker for anything small and cuddly. But dogs were a responsibility. She looked at Riley, expecting him to say so. He looked back—as starry-eyed as Jake.

"He really is swell, Mom," Jake said again. His eyes beseeched her. Then he turned his gaze on Riley. "Isn't he?"

"So's this one," Riley said, nodding at the bundle of fluff he held. He stroked the pup's head and silky back.

Dori, watching, despaired of them both. She looked at Maggie and saw the other woman grinning all over her face. Dori sighed.

Robert Tanner laughed. "The pups are too young to leave their mother," he told Jake. "But if you and Riley are still interested in a few weeks..."

Jake beamed. He took the pup out of Dori's hands, holding him gently, nuzzling his neck. "Did you hear that, Tugger?"

"Tugger?" Dori and Riley repeated together.

Jake colored. "He just, um, looks like a tugger," he said.

"I think it might be time for you to put Tugger and his brothers and sisters back with their mom," Maggie suggested. "They're pretty little yet. They'll get tired. And it's almost time for us to start eating. You guys are hungry, aren't you?"

Oh, my, yes, they were.

It was a lovely afternoon for a barbecue. Dori enjoyed it thoroughly. She liked the people she met—the ranchers and their wives, the cowboys, the teachers and townspeople. They were friendly and welcoming—even Jeff Cannon as the day wore on. It was her dream come true.

She began to feel as if she'd been transported to her very own version of Eden.

And then she began to recognize the snake.

Tricia Cannon, Dori realized at some point during the evening, was the girl with Riley in the picture in Jake's bedroom.

It had been taken back in high school, and after a brief initial curiosity, Dori had looked past it. She, after all, had gone to the prom with Biff Mallett in high school. And if there had ever been an unmemorable occasion in her life, that was it.

She had assumed Riley felt the same way, that perhaps he'd

just saved the picture because it was the last time he'd worn a suit.

But she didn't think so anymore.

Because there was something still going on between him and Jeff Cannon's wife.

Not an *affair*.

Dori could tell right away that they weren't having an affair. There was no false heartiness or smooth banter designed to disguise a more intimate relationship. There was just... awareness.

Everywhere Riley went, Tricia Cannon's eyes seemed to follow him.

At first Dori had thought *she* was the one Tricia was watching, that the other woman was curious about her because she was "the new girl." But then she realized that Tricia's eyes were on her only when she was with Riley.

And Riley watched Tricia as well.

No matter where he was, who he was talking to, or what he was doing, he seemed to know where Tricia was, too. Or if he lost sight of her for a moment, he scanned the groups of people until he found her. Then something in his body seemed to settle, to focus.

He loved her.

Suddenly Dori understood what he'd meant when he'd said he would never marry.

Of course he wouldn't—because the woman he loved was already married—to someone else!

Something hard and tight seemed to take a grip on Dori's midsection. She watched Riley watching Tricia, and deep inside she felt an ache begin to grow. She swallowed, breathed deeply, tried to ease the tightness in her throat. But it wouldn't go away.

Sam Gallagher's wife, Sue, came up to her. "I'm so glad you're with Riley now," she said.

Dori jumped, startled. "I'm not—" she began. "I mean, I'm not *with* Riley. Not like...not like..."

"It's early days yet," Sue said with a light laugh.

"I don't think Riley is...interested." Her gaze went from

Riley to the woman he was watching, though he appeared to be talking to the Walker brothers.

Sue followed her gaze. She snorted. "Riley was imprinted at an early age."

So everyone knew about him and Tricia? Dori supposed she shouldn't be surprised. It was a small community, after all.

Now she smiled. "Like a duck, you mean?"

"Like a jerk," Sue corrected. "And now he doesn't know any better. He thinks Tricia is the only woman in the world. We're hoping you'll change that."

"I don't think—"

"Do you like him?" Sue pressed the issue.

"Of course, I—"

"Don't just do that polite, 'of course I like him' business. Riley's a hunk, don't you think?"

Dori ran her tongue over her lips. She debated her responses. Finally she decided on honesty. "Yes."

Sue beamed, justified. Then her smile faded as she seemed to consider something. "You loved his brother."

"Yes." Dori was honest there, too. "But not—"

"Not like Riley."

"Riley and I aren't—"

"Not yet."

"Don't get your hopes up," Dori warned.

"Get *yours* up," Sue said. "You're not going to get him otherwise."

Dori didn't know what to say to that. For all that she had fallen in love with him and was willing to admit it to herself, she wasn't admitting it to anyone else.

And she wasn't at all sure she would get him even if she did. While her little "experiment" the other night in the alcove had proved he was "interested," now she saw that it might have been only a matter of hormones on red alert.

Riley was a healthy male with all the normal instincts. He could react to a reasonably attractive female without caring a whit about her as a person. Men did.

Lots of men had—to her.

She smiled a little wanly at Sue, then said, "I think I'll see if Maggie could use some help in the kitchen."

Maggie didn't need any help in the kitchen. She said, "You should be out keeping Riley company."

Dori blinked. Had they had a community meeting before the barbecue? she wondered. Had they all got together and decided to shove her down Riley's throat?

"You're not 'matchmaking' by any chance?" she asked.

Maggie smiled. "Just wishing."

"Probably not a good idea."

But clearly her protests fell on deaf ears. Maggie let things ride during dinner, but after, when everyone was visiting, she said, "I think a little music and dancing would be a good idea."

She didn't seem to have checked this out with her husband ahead of time. Dori thought Robert looked as surprised as everyone else. But Billy Warren, Ev's grandson, was right there with a boom box and a stack of CDs, so Maggie must have clued someone in.

The music was light-and-lively, toe-tapping stuff that made Dori itch to move her feet. But she wouldn't have if Maggie hadn't said, "Everyone dance with the one who brung 'em."

Dori looked around to see Maggie give Riley a shove in her direction. He looked momentarily panic-stricken. But a stern look from Maggie sent him heading toward her.

She looked away, trying to pretend disinterest, expecting that he would find something or someone to waylay him before he got there. But the next thing she knew a pair of pointy-toed boots stopped right in front of her.

She looked up into Riley's eyes, astonished. *He actually intended to dance with her?*

She hadn't considered it a possibility, despite Maggie's urging. In fact, Dori had never even danced with Chris. Of course Chris had always played the music wherever they had been, so she'd never expected to. But even if he had been available, she didn't think he would have. Dancing somehow wasn't Chris's style. She wouldn't have thought it was Riley's. But he wasn't moving away.

"Do you…?" She still hesitated.

"Do I dance?" A self-deprecating grin quirked the corner of his mouth. "Well, some people might not call it that, but I've been known to now and then."

Dori remembered the photo of a very young Riley with his arm around an equally young Tricia at another dance many years ago. "I wasn't implying you didn't," she said quickly. "I was just…surprised." *That you wanted to dance with me.* Of course she didn't say that.

"My daddy said a cowboy ought to be able to dance as well as he can ride." Riley sounded absolutely serious.

Dori's brows lifted.

Then his grin flashed again. "Strattons are liberated men."

And drop-dead-gorgeous men, too, Dori thought, especially when they smiled. And who was she to say no to a handsome man, especially *this* handsome man—the man she had fallen in love with.

*Be careful, Dori,* her rational mind cautioned her. *He could break your heart.*

But she already knew it was too late to be careful. She'd stopped being careful when she'd left Livingston and jumped into the unknown in an effort to preserve Jake's dreams. Sometime in the past few weeks, her own dreams had risen from the ashes, as well.

Those dreams involved Riley.

Dancing with him just brought them one step closer to being real.

*So, damn her heart and her fears, full speed ahead.* She held out her hands, and he drew her lightly into his arms.

She had always admired Riley's loose-hipped stroll. She had, since their arrival at the ranch, enjoyed the sight of his ease on horseback. Both on foot and on a horse, he had a natural easy grace that drew a woman's eye.

But it was nothing compared to the awareness she felt when he took her in his arms and danced with her.

It wasn't exactly "close dancing," but it was a lot closer than Dori expected. Just the feel of his hands on hers seemed erotically charged tonight.

Because of the way she felt about him? Because obviously Maggie and Sue and perhaps others were rooting for her and Riley to make it as a couple? Because of the wondering way Riley was looking into her eyes as they moved together in the Tanners' yard?

She didn't know.

She only knew she felt lost when the music stopped and sorry when Riley's hands dropped away from her.

And sorrier still a couple of dances later when he held Tricia in his arms.

Dori had thought he wasn't going to dance again. He hadn't danced after that first dance with her. He'd stood against the fence nursing a beer and talking with Noah Tanner, watching the boys playing ball in the field. Dori, flustered at how she'd felt, had excused herself and slipped into the house to breathe deeply and steady her pistoning heart.

The music began again, but she didn't care. She'd danced with the only man she wanted to dance with. That was enough.

But when she came back, two dances later, Trace Jackson was waiting. He held out a hand to her. "Ah, I was lookin' for you. Dance, pretty lady?"

She could hardly say no. So she took Trace's hand and let him lead her into an easy two-step. He grinned at her. She gave him a fleeting smile in return. But she had to concentrate on what she was doing in order not to step on his feet.

She did so, anyway, when she looked up to see Tricia Cannon in Riley's arms.

"Oh, sorry!" She gabbled, trying to get straightened out, to remember what she was supposed to be doing.

*Focus on your partner, honey,* her mother had always told her. *Don't pay attention to anyone else. It's not polite.*

True.

Impossible.

As much as she tried to concentrate on Trace, her gaze seemed relentlessly attracted to the sight of Tricia and Riley together.

They seemed like a perfect couple. Tricia was so small that the top of her head barely touched Riley's chin. She looked delicate—doll-like. And she seemed so…so…comfortable in his arms. As if she belonged there.

Dori remembered the high school picture on Jake's bedroom wall and guessed that Tricia *had* belonged in Riley's arms for quite some time.

When had they broken up? When Tricia had married Jeff?

Had she dumped Riley to marry another man?

Dori couldn't imagine.

Jeff Cannon was a handsome man in his own right. Even taller than Riley, with broader shoulders and a stubborn jaw, he was very attractive. Dori could see that he would appeal to some women.

But judging from the way Tricia was edging just a little closer to Riley as they danced, she still felt something for him.

What bothered Dori most was the thought that Riley still felt something for her.


He felt hot.

Wyoming nights were rarely scorchers, but this one was making Riley sweat. There were clouds building behind the Big Horns, raising the humidity, increasing the temperature.

Or maybe it wasn't the night at all.

Maybe it was the dancing.

He wasn't usually all that eager to dance, but it was such a great excuse to do what he'd been wanting to do. Hell, how often could a guy just put his arms around a woman in public? Especially a woman he'd been aching to put his arms around ever since…well, he couldn't even remember how long.

Certainly since he'd kissed her that night in the alcove.

God, yes, he'd been aching to touch Dori again since then.

He hadn't dared. There was a line there—a line that required commitment to cross. Riley had never been a man given to casual sex. He'd tried it a couple of times after Tricia. But there had always been something missing.

And he knew what it was.

Love.

Just thinking the word sent shivers down his spine and made the hair on the back of his neck stand right up straight.

Love made the difference.

It was Tricia he loved. Tricia he hadn't touched in a dozen years.

Why now? Why was she making him dance with her tonight?

It was bittersweet. It was like pressing his nose against the candy store window, looking in, knowing he could never have what was inside. And yet somehow, even as they danced, his mind kept drifting. He kept remembering how Dori had felt in his arms. She was taller than Tricia. Slender, but not tiny. She had seemed, somehow, to fit more naturally in his embrace.

He glanced over at where she'd been standing next to Maggie.

She wasn't there. He frowned and looked around wildly.

"What's the matter?" Tricia asked, looking up into his eyes and fluttering her thick, blonde lashes.

"N-nothing." But still he scowled. Had she gone inside? Was she with Jake? His eyes searched the small groups of people laughing and talking. And then, quite suddenly, she danced right past him—in the arms of Trace Jackson.

"Ow!"

"Oh, sorry." Riley grimaced and gave Tricia a quick apologetic smile. "Didn't mean to step on you. Must've got distracted."

"Hmm." Tricia gave him a searching look.

Out of sheer habit, Riley looked away.

"She's quite something," Tricia said suddenly.

"Huh? What? Who?"

Tricia laughed, a soft, musical laugh. "Your…not quite sister-in-law. Chris's lover. Who else?"

Riley felt the muscles in his jaw bunch. He watched Dori smiling at Trace. It set his teeth on edge. Trace was a good hand, but he had a thing for the ladies. Dori didn't need a man to lead her astray.

"She's a good person," he said firmly. He wasn't sure why he thought Tricia's description of Dori was somehow disparaging or why he thought she needed defending, but he did. "She's a great mother," he added.

"Of course she is," Tricia said diplomatically.

"You'd like her if you got to know her."

Tricia smiled up at him. She flashed those gorgeous dimples at him. "I'm sure I would."

"You would," Riley insisted, dancing Tricia closer to Dori.

And then the music ended and he dropped his hold on her and turned toward Dori. "Come on," he said abruptly. "I've got to get up early. It's time to go home."

# Nine

The rain on his face woke him.

Riley was not unaccustomed to raindrops falling on his head. It was part and parcel of life on the range. But it was not supposed to be part and parcel of life in the bunkhouse.

He blinked and sat up, swiping at his face, then yanking the blankets up and rolling over, attempting to bury himself beneath them.

But the rain was relentless. And the blankets—unlike the bedroll he used outdoors—weren't waterproof.

Hell.

He threw the covers aside, hauled himself up and reached for his jeans. Of course they were wet, too. So was his shirt. He muttered more obscenities as he stumbled over to the dresser and pawed through a drawer for dry clothes.

The whole damn roof seemed to be leaking like a sieve. It had been sheer good luck, apparently, that he hadn't been washed out before now.

And sheer bad luck that it was tonight—the night when he'd

gone to sleep remembering their dance earlier, remembering all too well what it had been like to hold Dori in his arms.

And Tricia, too, he reminded himself, surprised that he hadn't thought of her first. Hell, in one evening he'd held more women close than he had in the past dozen years.

He dragged on a dry pair of jeans, stuffed his feet into his boots, jerked on a shirt and slapped his hat on his head. Then he headed for the house.

It was three in the morning. He'd be up by five-thirty. Two and a half hours in the middle of the night—she'd never even know he'd used the couch.

Easing the back door open, Riley let himself in as quietly as he could. It was the first time he'd been in the house at night since Dori and Jake had arrived. He hadn't thought it would feel any different. It did. It felt…lived in. Homey. Warm.

Maybe it was the lingering scent of brownies from the pan that Dori had made yesterday afternoon. Maybe it was the stack of folded laundry on the kitchen table. *His* laundry, he realized. Clothes that Dori must have folded even after they'd come home last night, after he'd checked the horses and gone on to bed.

Dry clothes, he thought, feeling oddly grateful.

The ones he had put on to come into the house were damp from his sprint across the yard. He stripped them off now and pulled on dry ones. He tried not to think about her folding his briefs. He knew the thought would make him hard. Every time he thought about it, crazy as it was, he almost felt as if her hands had touched *him!*

He dragged a clean white T-shirt over his head, then draped his jeans and shirt on the kitchen chairs. Then he padded into the living room and contemplated the couch. It was long and narrow and it wasn't going to be very comfortable. He was in no hurry to stretch out on it.

He thought maybe he'd go back to the bathroom first. And on his way back, if he just happened to glance into Dori's room—*his* room, he reminded himself—well, maybe he could say he was looking for a pair of socks.

He went to the bathroom. He brushed his teeth. He contemplated his face in the mirror and ran a hand over his stubbled jaw. He looked a hell of a lot older than the kid he remembered who used to look in the mirror out of these same eyes. Where had the years gone?

Where had his life gone?

What did he have to show for any of it?

*Go to sleep,* he told himself. *You never were a damn bit of good at this soul-searching business. There's no point to it.*

And there wasn't. There was only living day to day. Getting by. Trying not to think about the years, about the past, about all the dreams he'd once had.

What was wrong with him tonight was that those dreams seemed to be rising from the dead, drifting up out of the ashes, stirring to wakefulness. They made him want—

*No, no, they didn't. Don't think about it,* he told himself. *Go to sleep.* He flicked out the light and headed for the living room.

But first he had to stop and look at Dori.

He'd never seen Dori asleep.

He had no right to look at her now. He couldn't help himself.

He stood in the doorway to his room—now hers—and gazed in. There was no moonlight to help him. No stars. He had to step in, to go closer, to step aside and let the tiny bit of light reflected from the nightlight in the bathroom spill across her face.

She was beautiful. Of course he'd always known that. Chris would never have looked twice at her if she hadn't been.

No, he admitted to himself, that wasn't exactly true. Dori had an innate sweetness about her that would have made her beautiful—even to Chris. Was that what had attracted his brother?

Riley didn't want to think about it.

He didn't want to think about Dori and his brother. Didn't want to remember that she'd loved his brother.

"Mmm."

The soft sound from the bed made him jerk, afraid that she was awakening. But she only smiled a little and hugged her pillow closer. She'd never held him that close, Riley thought.

And she never would.

*Get out of here! Now. Don't think things like that. Don't want things like that!*

He didn't want them, he assured himself as he beat a retreat to the couch. He didn't.

It was Tricia he loved.

It was Dori, though, who spent the night in his dreams.


She awoke at six. The skies were lead-gray, and Dori could hear rain on the roof. There was a chill in the air, and even though she knew that winter came early in these parts, she didn't think it ought to arrive in August. But the rain might be snow at higher elevations. She got up and pulled on a robe, then went to look out the window.

She wondered when Riley had begun moving cattle this morning. He had talked about getting an early start.

"Don't bother fixin' me breakfast," he'd said last night on their way home. He'd been polite, almost formal. The man who had danced with her scant hours earlier, seemed to have vanished into thin air.

Of course he had, she reminded herself, once he'd danced with Tricia Cannon.

Riley and Tricia.

She'd wondered if he might say something about it—them!—explain a little on the way home. But of course he hadn't.

Further reflection had made her realize that he never would. Feelings were one thing Riley never talked about. And feelings for another woman—especially unrequited feelings—were so far off the list of conversational topics that she might as well expect the stardust cowboy to come sit on her bed and sing "Home on the Range" just for her.

Riley and Tricia.

*Damn it, don't!* She sighed and tried not to. Heartbreak wasn't something she wanted to go looking for.

She was afraid it would find her soon enough.

She stuffed her feet into a pair of moccasins, scuffed out

down the hall to put on some coffee—and stopped dead at the sight of Riley sound asleep on the couch.

What the—?

Bare calves and feet stuck out below one end of a small afghan. He had the other end clutched against his T-shirt-clad chest. Most of it, however, was dangling off the couch and onto the floor, leaving her a very good view of Riley in his briefs.

Instantly Dori looked away, embarrassed at the direction of her gaze.

Almost as quickly, she looked back.

"You've got to trust your instincts, Dor'," Milly had insisted when Dori was driving away from Livingston to an unknown future.

So, fine, she was trusting her instincts.

She couldn't help it that they were base! It wasn't often she had a chance to stand there and look her leisure at a barely clad man. Especially this man.

Riley shifted in his sleep. So did the contents of his briefs. He was—Dori swallowed—large.

Men were. When they slept, they, er…grew. It was academic. It had nothing to do with sexual excitement. Of course she knew that. Still…

She pressed her hands to suddenly warm cheeks. And then she took a step backwards, stumbled, bumped into the lamp and—

"Huh! Wha—?" Riley's eyes jerked open as Dori groped for balance.

"I—you—" Her face was flaming. She could feel it. "It's past six," she managed at last. "What are you—"

He sat up, yanking the afghan around his waist with one hand, raking his fingers through his hair with the other. "Cripes! I must've—"

"What are you—?"

"The roof leaks. I came in and fell asleep and— Hell." He stumbled to his feet and, clutching the afghan around him, he headed toward the bathroom. "I gotta get going."

Dori heard the door bang. She stood rooted to the spot, her cheeks still aflame.

Then she heard the door open again. "Dori?"

"What?"

"Hand me my clothes, will you?"

He went out in the rain to check on the cattle.

"When I come back, I'll fix the roof," he promised on his way out the door. He *had* to get that roof fixed.

He didn't want to even think about waking up to find Dori standing over him on the couch again! Cripes, why had he overslept like that?

Well, it wouldn't happen tomorrow. Tomorrow he'd be back in the bunkhouse.

In the meantime, he spent the day remembering what she'd looked like sleeping—trying to forget she'd seen *him* sleeping! And he came home early, determined to climb up on the roof to nail down something to cover the leaks.

Dori had moved his gear back into the house.

"You did what?" He stared at her, astonished.

"It was ridiculous for you to be out there, anyway," she said matter-of-factly. "Entirely unnecessary. There's a perfectly good bed in Jake's room, if you won't let me give you back your own."

"I won't," he said flatly.

"So I put your things in with Jake's."

"It'll be swell, Riley," Jake said with enormous good cheer. "You'll see. You'll be glad you're there."

In fact Riley went to bed with mixed feelings.

Yes, he was dry. And yes, the bed was more comfortable by far than the one he'd slept on in the bunkhouse. And Jake was a much better roommate than Chris had ever been. Neater, for one thing. Less sulky. And very eager to whisper confidences to Riley after the lights were out.

"You're supposed to be asleep," Riley told him when Jake started whispering to him when he came to bed.

"Kids don't need as much sleep as grown-ups think they do."

"How do you know?"

"I'm awake, aren't I?"

There was no answer to that. Riley slid between the crisp sheets of the bottom bunk. "You oughta be sleepin'," he said gruffly.

"I will," Jake promised. "Pretty soon."

Riley heard him shift in the top bunk, then saw the curtain pulled aside.

"He's up there." Jake's voice was quietly confident.

Riley rolled onto his side and punched his pillow. "What're you talkin' about?"

"Him." Jake pulled the curtain back further. "The stardust cowboy."

Riley groaned. "You're not gonna start up on that again, are you? It's just a story."

"I know that," Jake said impatiently. "But that doesn't make it not true." He bounced a little in the bunk above. "I'm here, aren't I? An' I'm gettin' Tugger, aren't I?" He leaned out of the bed and hung his head upside down to look at Riley in the darkness.

Riley scowled. "What else are you dreamin' about?" he muttered.

"Can't tell," Jake said. "Won't happen if I do."

Riley raised up on one elbow. "Listen, Jake, things…don't always happen if you dream 'em." He didn't want to destroy the boy's confidence, but he did want him to be a little realistic.

Jake's head bobbed. "I know. But…some things are just meant to happen. Like me comin' here. You know what I mean?" There was such earnestness in his young voice that Riley couldn't deny him.

"I know," he said, and it was true. There was a rightness about Jake's having come. For all that Riley hadn't wanted anything of the sort in the beginning, now he couldn't imagine not having Jake living there.

Or Dori, either.

He didn't want to think about that. Dori confused him, made him feel things he hadn't felt in years, made him want things he didn't have any business wanting. And he knew he'd be wanting them more than ever, now that he was sleeping just across the hall from her.

"I know," he said to Jake again, gruffly because his throat felt oddly tight. "Now go to sleep or I'll be sorry you did come."

Whatever had gone on between Riley and Tricia, it wasn't over.

Dori was sure of it.

Especially when Tricia called several days after the barbecue to invite them over for dinner. And if the invitation said a lot— the actual evening they spent with Tricia and Jeff confirmed it.

It wasn't blatant. Tricia didn't throw herself at Riley. But she touched him. She passed him in the doorway between the living room and the dining room, and her breasts brushed against Riley's arm. She managed to touch him when she was passing dishes during mealtime, too. Her hand lingered on his arm when she told a funny story and somehow just needed to touch someone to make a point.

She even ruffled his hair once when she passed him sitting by Jake near the fireplace. It appeared to be a casual movement. But Dori saw Riley jump and knew it wasn't casual to him.

Riley was as aware of Tricia as she was of him.

Dori was aware of both of them.

Jeff didn't seem aware of anything at all. Except business. He apologized profusely for his distraction. "I didn't realize Tricia had already invited you," he said after they'd eaten, "and I'd already made arrangements for a conference call this evening. I hope you'll excuse me."

Tricia pouted. "Jeff's so busy all the time. He never has a moment for me or the kids."

"That's not true," Jeff said. "Matt went with me to Chey-enne just last week."

"He never has a moment for me," Tricia corrected. She made a sound, which Dori supposed was intended to be a light laugh, but it came out sounding rather strained.

"A lawyer's work is never done," Jeff said.

"Like a cowboy's," Riley agreed.

But Tricia put her hand on his arm. "Oh, you always had time for me."

Riley stiffened and eased his arm out from her grasp. "That was a long time ago." He gave a quick laugh.

"A very long time ago," Jeff said firmly.

But Tricia lifted her chin. "Not so very," she said meaningfully. "Riley was extremely attentive in college." She smiled at her husband, then at Riley, then at last at Dori. There was a definite possessiveness in her tone.

Dori didn't say anything then. But once they were home and Jake was in bed, she tracked Riley down.

"Okay," she said. "Tell me what's going on."

Riley didn't know what was going on.

He didn't know what Tricia was trying to do. After a dozen years of her being married to another man, she was suddenly an issue in his life.

Well, actually, she'd always been an issue in his life. But up until the dance at Tanners' she'd been a *resolved* issue.

And now?

"What's going on?" Dori demanded again. "Between you and Tricia Cannon?"

"Nothin's goin' on!" He scowled fiercely at her. "What do you think?"

"I don't know what to think," she said flatly. "That's why I'm asking. The two of you have a past."

"We went out in high school. And college," he added grudgingly after a moment. Then, when she still waited, he scowled. "What? There's nothin' to tell!"

Dori's brow lifted, but she didn't say anything.

"Oh, hell," Riley muttered. "You want it blunt? I'll give it to you blunt. I wanted to marry her, and I thought she wanted to marry me. But I think she really wanted just to get out of here. Her old man was a pretty poor rancher, and all she could think was how great it would be to move to the city. When I went away to college, she thought I was her ticket out. She went, too. And in her mind we were gonna go together. Didn't matter to her that I always wanted to come back here and ranch.

She figured I'd smarten up soon enough. Trouble was, my mother died and my old man got hurt, and I ended up coming back a whole lot sooner than either of us figured. I asked her to come with me, but she wouldn't. She was going to finish school, she said. And—'' he shrugged ''—I thought she would come after that. Instead she found another guy. One she hoped would take her away. And Jeff did—for a while. They moved back about six years ago. They're here. So am I. It's no big deal. And that's all.''

"That's all," Dori echoed quietly. She seemed to be considering what he'd said, weighing it. And then she shook her head. "It doesn't seem as if that's all."

"Well, it is." Riley lifted his chin, daring her to argue.

They stared at each other.

And then she said quietly, "You love her."

"I *loved* her," Riley corrected.

"Does she love you?"

"Of course not!"

Dori just looked at him.

Riley jammed his hands in his pockets. "That's the stupidest thing I've ever heard! She's married! She's been married a dozen years. She isn't interested in me."

Dori didn't reply. But her eyes met his again, wide and questioning, still asking things that he couldn't begin to answer.

It was all in Dori's imagination. She was letting the local gossip color her interpretation of events. Riley told her so.

Even though he, too, was a little surprised that Tricia was suddenly calling him up, it made perfect sense for her to do so. Why shouldn't she call him and ask his advice about a horse she was thinking of buying for her son?

Jeff was no horseman. He wouldn't know the first thing about what to look for.

So Riley did what any good neighbor would do. He gave her the benefit of his expertise.

"Maybe you could come look at one or two with me...er, us, sometime?" she suggested.

"I reckon I might do that. Just got Jake a horse of his own," he added.

"I heard," she said. "That's why I thought of calling you."

Of course it was.

See, he told Dori, there was a perfectly reasonable explanation.

There was an equally reasonable explanation for her to call and tell him about a couple they used to know at school down in Laramie.

"She just wanted me to know that Lacey and Jim had a baby," he told Dori after he hung up that time.

"First child?" Dori asked.

"Hmm? No, fourth, I think."

"She called you about all of them?"

"I...don't remember," he said. He didn't think she had. But then he remembered. "The others were born when Tricia and Jeff were livin' down in Denver."

Dori just looked at him.

"It's true!"

But he knew she thought he was encouraging Tricia's calls. And perversely Tricia thought he was encouraging Dori.

"She's real pretty, Riley," Tricia had said more than once.

He hadn't denied it. Dori was pretty. He spent a lot of time thinking about just how pretty she really was. And since they'd danced—and kissed—he thought about other things, too. It surprised him sometimes how much time he spent thinking about her—even when Tricia was calling him.

"I'm beginning to think you're sweet on her, Riley." Tricia teased.

He bristled. "Don't be ridiculous. She was my brother's woman. I wouldn't go after another man's woman."

"No." Tricia said. "That's true." She sounded pleased.


He and Dori were in the middle of creating a screen saver when the phone rang.

Creating a screen saver was not Riley's idea of a great way to spend the evening. But it was pretty interesting—the alcove being as small as it was, and all. Whenever they moved, Dori's body tended to brush against his, her scent filled his nostrils, her voice teased his ears.

He couldn't have the woman he loved, but he found he was enjoying this one. He was even considering trying that kissing bit again.

And then the phone rang.

"Riley?" It was Tricia.

His body, already somewhat aroused from being near Dori, went on alert. He sat up straight. He moved his knee, which had been touching Dori's. "What's up?" He could feel Dori's eyes on him. He didn't look at her.

"I just wanted you to know I found a horse for Matt."

"That's great," he said.

"It's a seven-year-old bay gelding. Can you look at it to-morrow?"

"Don't reckon I can tomorrow. I got some haying to do in the morning. Then I'm goin' up on the Bureau land. Gotta move some cattle."

"I could bring him to you. Ride him. Meet you at the old swimming hole?"

Riley sat up straighter. *Meet him? At the swimming hole?* "Well, I—"

"About three," Tricia said firmly. "You could be there by three, couldn't you?"

"I...I guess. But—"

"Perfect," she said. "I'll see you then. Thanks, hon'." And she was gone.

*Hon'?* She'd called him *hon'?*

"Who was that?" Dori asked when he hung up.

"Uh...Tricia," he said, distracted.

Dori stopped looking at the computer and stared at him.

"She found a horse for Matt. Wanted me to look at him." He got up from the computer and moved away into the bed-room, edgy now, his thoughts whirling. He rubbed a hand over his hair. *The swimming hole? Tricia wanted to meet him at the swimming hole?*

"Can we skip that screen saver thing tonight? I'm bushed. Reckon I'll pack it in now and get an early start in the morning.

It's a long ride. If I do the haying first, I probably won't be back till supper.''

Dori didn't say anything for a moment. Then she nodded. "Fine,'' she said. "All right. Whatever you want.''

All day long he considered not meeting Tricia.

It wasn't as if she really needed his approval of a horse for her boy. If she was confident enough of the horse to ride it all the way out there, it couldn't be too bad an animal.

But then he thought maybe it would be a good opportunity to talk to her, to find out—now that she'd had a chance to get to know Dori—what she thought of Jake's mother.

He wasn't sure why it mattered. She hadn't asked *him* what he'd thought of Jeff, for heaven's sake!

But it wouldn't hurt to see her. So when he finished checking the cattle up on the Bureau land, he made his way down to the swimming hole around three.

A quick glance around told him that Tricia wasn't there yet. He sat waiting on his horse, glanced at his watch, then dismounted, loosened the cinch on his saddle and left his horse to graze by the trees. If he was going to have to wait, he'd move closer to the water where it was cooler.

Three turned into three-thirty. Riley shifted uncomfortably on the rocks. Looking at the pond made him remember all the times he'd been here with Tricia. And his body remembered things even better than his mind did.

He eased the fit of his jeans and tried not to remember anymore.

But then he started thinking about Dori having been here with Jake. Of course she wouldn't have gone swimming in her birthday suit. Not with her son around. But in Riley's mind, Jake wasn't around. And in his head he could imagine Dori— all that rosy skin naked and gleaming as she stood in the pond and beckoned to him.

Damn!

He jumped to his feet and began to pace, glancing at his watch, wondering if Tricia had forgotten how long it took to get there. He glanced at his watch and wondered if she was coming at all.

He wasn't going to sit here waiting forever. Not when Dori was all alone back at the ranch.

He'd give her until four-fifteen. An hour and a quarter was enough time.

At quarter past four, he gave up.

And breathed a sigh of relief.

She wasn't coming. She'd thought better of it. She'd decided she didn't need Riley's opinion of her boy's new horse. She'd decided she didn't need to get any more involved with Riley than she had been the past twelve years.

And she was right.

Very very right. He got to his feet and looked around one last time. No Tricia.

Only memories.

Memories that—before he went back to the ranch house and Dori—he needed to erase.

He yanked off his boots and socks, shed his shirt and jeans and shorts and plunged into the icy water.

Shivering, he broke the surface. His body hated him. His mind approved. Teeth chattering, he ducked down again. He swam across the pond, then turned and started back.

He was halfway there when he glanced up—and saw Tricia standing on the bank watching him.

She was standing right at the water's edge, smiling at him the way he remembered her smiling at him all those years ago right before she'd shed her clothes and walked straight into his arms.

Riley stopped dead and stood up. The water lapped his waist.

"I'm glad you waited. What a good idea." Her words were sultry and her hands went to the buttons of her shirt.

Riley stared, aghast. "What the—! Where've you— *Don't do that!*"

Tricia's hands stilled. Her lips pouted, and she looked at him, baffled. "What? Don't do what?"

"*That!*" he yelped when she started again. "Don't do *that!* Stay right there! I'll come out." And then he realized he couldn't. Not as long as she was standing there waiting for him!

She realized it, too, and grinned. It was a damned seductive grin. "Come on, then." Her laugh was musical, beckoning, tempting.

He didn't move. "Don't be stupid," he retorted.

"You don't want to swim with me, Riley?" There was a soft, teasing note in her voice.

His face burned. "Cut it out, Trish. You didn't show up. I waited. I got hot. I—"

"I bet you did."

"It was hot, so I took a swim," he said fiercely. "Now go away—over beyond the trees and let me get dressed and I'll look at your horse."

"It's a good horse," she said. But she still didn't move, just stood there, eyes on him.

Riley glared. "Let me get out and let me see him, then."

Tricia's smile widened. She opened her arms. "Anytime you're ready, sweetheart."

"Don't play games, Tricia."

The smile faded, but still she didn't move. "I'm not playing games, Riley."

Checkmate. He couldn't get out. She wouldn't go away.

Then finally she said, "You're right. It is hot." And then, damned if she didn't start unbuttoning her shirt again!

"Trish! Stop it! Don't do that! Cripes!" He was torn between shutting his eyes and staring in fascination as she bared her creamy skin right in front of him.

His mouth went dry. "Stop!" he said again hoarsely.

But she just smiled at him. She didn't stop. She stripped off every stitch—shimmied out of her jeans, flung her shirt and bra aside, then peeled down her panties and kicked them away.

Riley's tongue seemed glued to the roof of his mouth. He couldn't take his eyes off her. It had been years—*years!*—since he'd seen her naked. Her body was fuller now, lusher than he remembered. She was still small, delicate, but there was a womanly look to her now.

And—omigod!—a womanly feel, too, which he discovered

when she walked right out into the water and put her arms around him!

He jerked back, pushing her away. "Trish! For God's sake! Don't!"

She fluttered her lashes and pouted at him. "Why not?"

He was backpedaling as fast as he could. "You can't! You're married!" But it didn't seem to matter to her. She came after him again. "Don't do this!"

She caught his arm and pressed close. "Why not?" she asked again, looking up at him, eyes wide and luminous. "You want me, Riley. You know you do."

Well, his body did, at least. And there was ample evidence to prove it. But still Riley shook his head.

"No! I don't," he insisted. "And you don't either, damn it. You're married!"

"Tell Jeff that," she said with a hint of bitterness.

Riley frowned. "What's that mean? Jeff knows. He loves you." That much at least Riley was certain of.

Tricia made a face. "Not the way you do."

*Do.* Not *did.* Riley shook his head. "Of course I love you," he said. He would always love her for the girl she had been, the couple they had once been. But—

"So love me now," she said, snuggling close again.

"Trish! No! You're married! You're just…goin' through some phase or somethin'. This isn't real. You know it isn't!" He peeled her hands away and held her out at arm's length, looking down into her eyes. "Go on home, Tricia. Now. You're out of your head!" Then he let her go and prayed she'd turn and walk away.

Instead her hands dipped below the water's surface, seeking him, finding him.

"No!" Riley jerked back and shoved her away—hard—so hard that she sat right down in the water, while he turned and swam as fast as he could toward the far side of the pond.

Sputtering, Tricia got to her feet. She slapped her hands on her hips and glared at him. Jaw locked, Riley stared back.

Then she said, "Well, if that's the way you want it, Riley Stratton…"

And she turned and stomped back to shore.

Riley took a deep, shuddering breath and turned his back. He didn't watch her go. He was just damned glad she had.

He kept his back turned as he listened to the sounds of her dressing, then mounting the horse and heading out. Then the horse seemed to stop.

"You're a son of a bitch, you know that, Riley?" Tricia shouted back at him.

Yeah, he knew it.

He shut his eyes. His chest heaved. His body ached. His mind spun. *Get a grip,* he told himself. *The worst is over.* She'd come. She'd gone.

He'd survived.

There was nothing worse that could happen.

He waited until he was sure she was far away before he finally made his way out of the water.

That's when he discovered his horse—and his clothes—were gone, too.

# Ten

## ———

**A**ll day long Dori jumped every time she heard a noise, hoping it was Riley returning home.

Of course, she told herself, it wasn't likely. He had made a point of saying that he had to go up to the BLM land. She knew when he went that way he rarely returned early. Still...

Still she hoped.

Jake would be at Tanner's all day and all night. Maybe Riley would come back early. She did the laundry, changed the sheets on everyone's bed, entertained herself with a fantasy of Riley sharing her bed—*his* bed—with her. It was a lovely fantasy, embroidered, as it was, with snatches of remembered glimpses of Riley with his shirt unbuttoned, Riley with his jeans barely zipped, Riley bare-chested, coming out of the bathroom toweling his hair dry. He hadn't seen her any of those times.

But she'd seen him.

Sometimes she wondered if she simply managed to be in the vicinity when he was coming out of the bathroom from taking a shower, or if her subconscious was making her go in that direction. Whichever…the glimpses were a treat.

They made her want more.

A lot more.

They made her want *all* of Riley.

She had started again to dream.

But it was getting later and later. The nice dinner she'd put on was going to be dried out by the time he got home. So much for dreams.

She had stopped dreaming and was glancing outside for any sign of him when the phone rang.

It was Milly. Milly and Dori had had weekly conversations since Dori had left. Mostly they talked about Jake and the ranch. But somehow Riley's name came up. Milly always wanted to know about Riley.

"Is he like Chris?" she'd asked the first time they'd talked.

"Not…very," Dori had said.

"Better?" Milly had been hopeful.

"I'm not going to make comparisons," Dori had replied starchily.

"Yes," Milly had translated.

Since then she'd asked about him, but not too often. "I'm dying to know what's going on, but I don't want to jinx anything."

"There's nothing to jinx," Dori had protested at first. "Honestly, Milly." But now that she was dreaming, she wasn't protesting anymore.

"Are you happy?" Milly asked her now.

Still looking out the window, Dori replied. "Yes. I'm happy. Of course I am."

Something of the caution she felt must have been clear in her voice, for Milly didn't press further. She said, "Good. I knew you made the right move. And actually I think it's been good for Dad, too."

"How?" Dori was almost afraid to ask. She had had only the briefest of stilted conversations with her parents since she and Jake had left Livingston.

"He's…kind of quiet," Milly said. "Like he's thinking about things."

"I'm not sure that's good."

"You'd have to be here to understand," Milly told her. "I think you made him pause for thought."

"Swell."

"It might be." Milly was ever the optimist.

"So—" Dori changed the subject "—when are you and Cash getting married?"

"After shipping. Then you and Riley and Jake can come."

Not "you and Jake and Riley," Dori noticed. Somehow Riley had got in the middle—as if he were part of the family.

"Well, Jake and I—"

"All of you," Milly insisted. "I never even got to meet him. I want to."

"But—" But Dori didn't argue too hard. She hoped. And then she glanced out of the window again. By the corral she saw a movement. She pushed back the curtain and caught a glimpse of Riley's horse. Saddled.

But no Riley.

"What the—?"

"What's wrong?" Milly asked her.

"Nothing. I—" Dori craned her neck, trying to see where Riley was. "I don't know. I just saw Riley's horse and—"

"Where there's a horse, there's Riley. Well, I'll let you go, then. Have fun," Milly said with considerable cheer and just a hint of something naughty in her tone.

Dori hung up the phone and went to the door to look again.

There was no Riley.

The sun was getting low in the sky when Riley finally heard the sound of hooves. He'd been sitting there for, he reckoned, close to three hours, fuming and furious—as much at himself as at Tricia.

At least she'd come back. He'd begun to get worried. He'd been trying to imagine walking all the way back to the ranch in the dark clad in only his boots.

The trek, he figured, wouldn't be as difficult as explaining to Dori how he happened to get into the situation in the first place.

Thank God now he wouldn't have to!

The sound of the hooves came closer. "Riley?"

"Over—!" he began and then realized the voice calling him wasn't Tricia's.

"Over where?" Dori called back.

Damn it! She'd heard him. He plunged back into the water, shivering as its icy cold bit into exposed body parts.

"Riley! Where are you? Are you hurt? Can you hear me?"

He saw her now through the trees. The horse was clopping through the creek, and coming out the other side, heading straight for him. Dori was looking all around, frantic.

Hell, *she* was frantic! What about *him?*

"Riley! *Riley, where are you?*"

He wanted to die. Maybe he could drown. Could you will yourself not to come to the surface and take a breath?

He didn't have time to find out. She spotted him.

"What the—!" She flung herself off her horse and took half a dozen steps toward where he stood, chest deep in the water and wishing he could drown. "What are you doing?"

He opened his mouth. No sound came out.

"Are you all right? Do you have a cramp? Your horse came back to the house. I've been looking everywhere. Yelling. I thought you'd been hurt." She was babbling. Nervous. Standing on the water's edge now, looking at him, confused, curious.

Riley shut his eyes, as if not seeing her would make her disappear. But when he opened them again, she was still there. Still looking worried. Frantic.

And gorgeous. Wonderful. Ten times better than Tricia ever had.

If *Dori* had come into the water after him today, he wouldn't have pushed *her* away.

He wanted to walk straight out of the water now, lay her down and make love to her right there.

"Riley," she demanded, her tone urgent, "what's the matter with you?"

"C'mere." His voice was ragged, as urgent as hers, and he

was as astonished by what he'd just said as she appeared to be.

She goggled at him. "What?"

He gave a quick desperate shake of his head. "Nothin'. I…I—" But there were no words. Nothing at all could express the tumult of feelings surging through him.

Oh, God.

"Are you stuck?" she demanded.

Well, that was one way of looking at it. He just looked at her mutely. There was no way out and he knew it. He sighed.

"*Riley, what is the matter with you?* What are you doing in there?"

He drew a breath and told himself to get it over with. "I was hot. The weather was hot," he corrected, remembering he'd used those words to Tricia. "So I decided to take a swim." He stopped, hoping she would just say, *Oh, that's nice,* and leave it there.

She didn't say anything. She just waited. "And," she prompted finally.

Hell. "So I did. I swam. And, uh, while I was swimming, I…um…lost my horse. And my clothes." This last was no more than a mutter.

She heard him anyway. Now her eyes really did get wide. She looked around quickly, as if ascertaining the truth of what he'd said. As if he'd lie about it, for God's sake! Then her gaze returned to him. She gaped. "You *lost* your clothes." It was a question, and it wasn't a question. There was a glimmer of something in her eyes that he didn't want to put a name to.

He grunted, eyeing her belligerently. She eyed him right back. He wasn't cold anymore. The heat of her gaze, combined with his own embarrassment, would turn the old swimming hole into a hot spring before too long!

"I didn't lose 'em intentionally," he said gruffly.

She cocked her head. "Oh." She seemed to be weighing that. Then she said, "How? How did you lose your clothes?"

"A rat ran off with them," he said through his teeth.

Dori's mouth twitched into a grin. "A rat?"

Riley scowled. "A rat." Only a rat would do this to him.

Dori looked around again. "The, um, rat…didn't take your boots."

"Prob'ly couldn't carry 'em."

"Or maybe it wanted you to be able to walk home."

Riley gritted his teeth. "Maybe."

"Not a very nice rat." She cocked her head. "Did you do something to the rat?"

He sucked in a breath. This was not something he wanted to talk about. But Dori clearly did. She was waiting for his answer, all ears.

Riley sighed. "Tricia came up when I was swimmin'. She…had this, um…idea…" He *definitely* did not want to talk about this!

But Dori was completely still, listening to every word he said. She didn't take her eyes off him, either.

"She thought she'd…go swimmin' with me." He didn't look at Dori.

"Swimming," she echoed. It wasn't quite a question, either, but there was a hell of a lot of skepticism in it.

"Swimming," he repeated. "And other things," he added in a mutter.

"Ah."

He could tell she knew what "other things" were. "I didn't do it," he said. "I would never do it. She's a married woman, for cryin' out loud! So I told her no."

"And she stole your clothes."

He colored fiercely. "She was mad," he explained, feeling like an idiot. "She sort of…came on to me and I sort of…pushed her."

Dori's eyes got saucerlike. "You pushed her?"

He shrugged. "She fell down in the water. She got wet. Not hurt. An' she got mad, I guess, too."

"I guess," Dori said dryly. Then she grinned. She laughed. Riley glared at her. "It's not funny!"

Dori wiped her eyes. "Of course not," she said, but she couldn't quite wipe the grin off her face. She hiccuped she was trying so hard not to laugh anymore. Her breasts jiggled when she laughed. Wasn't she wearing a bra today, either?

Riley sucked air.

"So, now what?" Dori said when she could finally manage a sentence again.

"You're ridin' Jake's horse. There should be a towel in the saddlebag." Thank God Jake had taken to being fastidious enough to bring a towel along because, he said, his body felt "squirmy" if he had to get back into his clothes when he was wet.

At the time Riley had shaken his head in disbelief. Now he understood all about "squirmy."

"Get me the towel," he said.

For a moment Dori didn't move. She was staring at him blankly. Her gaze seemed to have dropped to where the water lapped his midriff—and below. She couldn't see beneath the surface of the pond, could she? Riley dropped his hands.

"The towel?" he said impatiently.

"Huh? Oh—" she ran her tongue over her lips "—sure." She got the towel. It was a bath towel, but not a terribly big one. Still, Riley reckoned it would cover the essentials.

"Toss it to me."

Obediently Dori balled it up and threw it. The towel unfurled in flight—and landed in the water.

"Oh—" Dori pressed her fingers to her mouth "—dear!"

Riley added a few other four-letter words to that. He snatched the sopping towel up and dragged it around his waist. It billowed beneath the water, then settled against sensitive parts of his anatomy. It—*he!*—poked out like a damn tent pole! He stared down in dismay.

"Can I help?" Dori asked after a moment when he didn't move.

"No!"

"Sorry. I was just…wondering." She gave him a worried look. "What's wrong?"

"You know damn well what's wrong."

She hesitated, then a faint smile touched her mouth. "Oh," she said. "That." She looked away for a moment, then straight back at him.

"For…me?" she asked almost hesitantly.

He frowned, not sure what she meant.

So she spelled it out. "You. Um. Your…enthusiasm." Her gaze dropped to the part of him beneath the towel, below the water's surface, and her color deepened. "Is it for me…as opposed to…Tricia, I mean?" Her voice was tiny, almost distant. She didn't look him in the eye.

He almost smiled. "Yeah, it's for you," he admitted, his tone gruff.

Her gaze lifted, met his again. "Then I don't mind a bit." She held out a hand in his direction.

Still Riley hesitated.

"Riley," she said softly, insistently, "Come on."


Dori had ridden double before.

She'd ridden behind her brother, Deke, when, as a college student, he'd worked for Will Jones. She remembered putting her arms around his waist to hold on and keep her balance. More recently she'd ridden the same way with Jake. She'd sat with his small body pressed back against hers, holding him close.

It wouldn't be any different with Riley, she'd assured herself when he'd reached down and hauled her up behind him onto Jake's horse.

But there was something about riding double with a naked man…

Well, he wasn't entirely naked.

He had on boots. And a towel.

But the towel didn't do much, except cover the essentials from worldly view. She hadn't been polite enough to look away when he'd swung into the saddle. After all those fantasies brought on by handling his briefs, she wasn't about to miss a glimpse of the real thing when she had the chance!

Riley Stratton was very…impressive. His prolonged contact with cold water had not dampened his enthusiasm a great deal. He seemed pretty uncomfortable right now, from the way he was shifting around in the saddle.

"You okay?" She adjusted her grip on his bare waist, trying

not to bother him as he tried to get settled. The horse side-stepped, unused to the weight of two adults. "I can walk."

"No." His reply was a mutter. The horse sidestepped again. Dori slipped. She grabbed for something to hold on to. "Jeez!"

"Oops! Sorry! I didn't mean—" She let go of *that* as fast as she could. She locked her hands together around his middle. Doing so pressed her hard against his bare back, but it was better than...well, not *better* than...but *safer*...than what she had grabbed on to.

"Go," she said. "Let's go. We need to get home."

Riley touched his boots lightly to the horse's sides. The horse moved forward. Dori's breasts moved against Riley's back. Her hands pressed against his abdomen. Her thighs bounced against the backs of his bare legs.

"Yesssss," he said through his teeth. "We need to get home. Yesssss."


Riley had heard that foreplay was good. He'd read it in a magazine once. "Prolonged arousal heightens feelings, enhances awareness, makes for spectacular sex."

They never said anything about it damn near killing a man.

But then the experts probably didn't reckon that riding a horse naked with a woman's arms around you, rubbing you, touching you for the better part of five miles was foreplay.

They were wrong.

And it damn near killed him.

He'd wanted Dori Malone for weeks. He'd gone to bed aching with need every night just from looking at her, just from casually brushing past her in the alcove or from putting on a pair of Dori-folded undershorts. But it was nothing to how he felt now with her body pressed against his, mile after mile.

He could feel her cheek pressed against his back. Her breath teased his shoulder blade. And every once in a while, God help him, he thought he felt the touch of her tongue or her teeth there.

The first time he felt it, he almost jumped right out of the saddle. "What the—!" He jerked the reins so hard that Jake's horse shied and damned near bolted. He turned and glared at her.

Dori wetted her lips and looked back at him, all innocence. Except for that tiny flutter of a smile at the corner of her mouth.

"You askin' for trouble, Ms. Malone?"

She batted her lashes. "I don't know, Mr. Stratton. Am I?" Her raised chin grazed his back. Her hands smoothed the hard flesh of his belly, then slid fractionally lower. His towel twitched.

"You are playin' with fire," he warned her.

She dimpled. "Am I?" she asked again in a voice both innocent and sultry.

Riley sucked air. He shrugged bare loins against saddle leather trying to find ease. But there was no ease—only desire. A shudder ran through him. "Gotta get you home," he muttered.

Dori pressed her lips to his back. "A very good idea," she murmured.

He got her home. Barely.

He yanked off the saddle, turned the horse out and, clutching the towel with one hand and Dori with the other, he hobbled toward the house.

She opened the door. He shut it—and pressed her up against the wall.

"I'm dying," he muttered, his hips surging against hers, his face buried against her neck, his lungs gasping for air.

She turned her head, kissed his ear, nibbled it, nearly sending him over the edge. Then her hand found him. "You feel pretty lively to me."

He shook his head. "Don't! Not here. We gotta make it to a bedroom at least."

"We don't have to," she argued.

But he was having none of it. "Yes," he insisted, "we do. We waited this long. We can wait twenty seconds longer to do it right."

"Right isn't where," Dori told him, slipping her arms around him. "It's who."

He let go of the towel then. He scooped her up in his arms,

and somehow or other he got them down the hall. He stumbled on the rug, and they toppled headlong onto the bed. It creaked. It groaned. It didn't break.

He wouldn't have cared if it had.

It didn't matter.

Dori was right. What mattered wasn't where or when. What mattered was her.

He'd always thought he was a one-woman man. He'd always thought the woman was Tricia. Now he wasn't so sure.

Maybe he was still a one-woman man. But this was the woman.

Dori. She was the one he wanted. The one he thought about, dreamed about, cared about. Loved.

Yes, he did. He *loved* her.

She wasn't Tricia. She was sweeter than Tricia. Kinder than Tricia. Stronger than Tricia.

She'd come into his life and jarred him awake again. She'd made him sit up and look around, see the present and stop living in the past. She'd dared to take his plans and turn them upside down and inside out.

She'd given him Jake. And hopes. And dreams that he'd thought long dead.

He loved her.

He just hoped he could hang on five seconds at least and show her how much!

His fingers fumbled with her buttons. She helped. He couldn't manage the zipper of her jeans. She could. He didn't want to wait for her to take off her boots, but she made him. She made him wait until she was as naked—and far more gloriously beautiful in that nakedness—as he was.

Then she lay back on the bed and held out her arms to him.

For a split second he didn't move. He just looked at her—warm and welcoming, promising him more than he'd hoped for in a dozen years.

"Riley?"

He smiled. "Right here, darlin'." And then he slipped between her legs and let her guide him home.

His eyes shut. A shudder of sweet bliss swept through him

as he settled against her. He bit down on his lip, froze where he was, teetered on the edge, like some damn horny teenager too hot to control himself.

Her body tightened around him. She shifted her hips and somehow he seemed to slide in even deeper. He groaned.

"Riley?" She touched his face, stroked his hair.

"Ah, babe…" He kissed her jaw, her chin, her nose, her lips. They parted beneath his. Her tongue touched his. He trembled. *Steady, fella. Steady. Hold on. Hold back. Hold—*

And then she moved again. She rocked against him, tensed, rocked, tensed…rocked.

And he felt her body tighten, felt her quiver, felt her shatter. And he did, too.

His whole body shook as, warm and liquid, Dori wrapped him up and made him hers.

They loved again that night.

And again.

More times than Dori remembered. It didn't matter that she'd lost count.

What mattered was now and the future. She loved him. She knew that words were not Riley's medium. He didn't need to be told so much as he needed to be shown.

Earlier, right after the urgency of their first lovemaking had abated and they'd lain side by side in the tumbled bed, he'd risen up on an elbow and looked into her eyes. "I'm not Chris," he'd said quite seriously. "I can't ever be Chris."

She'd touched his chest, laid her palm against his heart, then had traced his lips and pressed a kiss where her fingers had lingered. "I don't want Chris," she'd told him. "I want you."

The look in his eyes had said he needed to believe that. So she'd shown him. She'd shown him with her kisses, with her touches, with her soft sounds and gentle nips. She showed him with everything that was in her. She gave him her body, her heart, her soul.

Later, after they dozed and awakened to each other again, he said he ought to take a shower.

"We could take one together," she responded.

He looked shocked. Then he grinned. It was the sexiest, heart-and-body-melting grin Dori had ever seen. And he took her hand and said, ''What a good idea.''

In the shower she lovingly washed him all over. Then she tried to hold still while he washed her.

''We could have done this at the swimming hole,'' she reminded him.

But Riley shook his head, nibbling her neck, caressing her back, cupping her buttocks and pulling her close. ''No,'' he murmured. ''Better here.''

He was right. It was. Just as he'd needed to know she wasn't confusing him with Chris, she had to be sure he wasn't thinking about Tricia.

He'd pushed Tricia away, she reminded herself.

He hadn't wanted Tricia. He wanted *her!*

And Dori wanted him. Desperately. His touches were driving her mad.

She snaked out a soapy hand and found him, teased him, stroked him. With her other she cradled the weight of him in her palm.

She heard him swallow and then he breathed raggedly against her ear. ''You tryin' to wring me out, woman?''

''I'm trying to love you. Too much for you, am I?'' she teased him.

A corner of his mouth tipped into a strained grin. ''We'll have to find out, won't we?'' He lifted her then, settled her legs on either side of his hips, and thrust deeply into her.

A sweet shudder rocked her. ''Oh, yes,'' she gasped. ''Let's.''

They did.


Riley was gonna be his father.

Jake was sure of it.

Oh, they hadn't told him yet. But he'd seen the way they looked at each other when he got back from Jared's. He saw the way they sometimes touched when they thought he wasn't paying attention.

He'd even seen Riley come up behind his mom when she

was sitting at the computer last night. He'd nuzzled at her ear and then he'd whispered something to her, and Jake had heard his mother laugh and turn her head and they had kissed.

Jake had taken a great deal of satisfaction from that kiss.

Now he pushed back the curtain and looked up at the star-studded sky. He remembered sitting in his mom's lap when he was so little she could pick him up without even thinking. He remembered looking at those stars while she told him stories about the stardust cowboy riding through the sky taking a little boy named Jake on wonderful adventures.

"Where do you want to go tonight?" she always asked him.

And Jake remembered bouncing up and down in her arms. "Wherever my daddy is," he said.

And his mom had wrapped her arms around him and touched him right where his heart was. "Your daddy's here, Jake."

That was true.

And Jake knew his flesh-and-blood dad was buried next to the set of grandparents he'd never known in town at the cemetery on the hill. But a part of his dad was in the stardust cowboy he'd written about—the cowboy who cherished hopes and dreams—and was determined to make them come true.

"You don't mind if Uncle Riley is my dad, too, do you?" he asked now, blinking up at the stars that winked back at him.

He took the wink to mean his father agreed. But just in case there was any question, any hesitation at all, Jake reassured him.

"It'll be okay," he told his father. "Mom says love is expandable. That means I can love you and Uncle Riley, too."


Word traveled fast.

Everybody seemed to know Riley was marrying Dori almost before Dori knew it herself.

She went into town two days later, and Gloria at the beauty shop said, "So when's the date?"

"Date?" Dori blinked. "For what?"

"The wedding, of course."

"Where you goin' on your honeymoon?" Sybil at the convenience store wanted to know.

"H-honeymoon?" Dori almost dropped the gallon of milk in her hand.

"Gotta have a honeymoon," Ev Warren poked the handle of a brand-new hammer at her. "Don't you let ol' Riley tell you he's gotta work so's he can't go. Everybody needs a honeymoon."

"Damn right," Robert Tanner nodded as he came up next to Ev and presented a united front.

Dori looked from one to the other of them. "Maggie?" she guessed. "Did Maggie tell you Riley and I were getting married?" Maggie had brought Jake home. She'd seen Dori's well-kissed mouth, Riley's unshaven cheeks and misbuttoned shirt.

Tanner shook his head. "I believe it was Jared who told me."

"And me," Ev agreed.

"Jared? How—" Dori winced. "Jake must have—" She would kill him.

She and Riley had talked about getting married, of course, the next night. They'd stepped guiltily around Jake's curious looks all day. But once he'd gone to bed, Riley had come to get her at the computer. He'd kissed her and drawn her up into his arms, and then he'd walked her out into the living room to do some talking.

"Not what I wanta do," he'd admitted. "But I reckon we got to talk. We'll get married," he'd said. He was kissing her. Little nibbling kisses that made her blood heat. "When do you want to get married?"

"Whenever you do." Her fingers had curled into fists in her lap.

"Doesn't matter to me." He had kept right on kissing. Then he'd taken her in his arms. "I have what I want."

Dori had tried to think straight. "M-maybe after shipping." She'd thought maybe they could get married when Cash and Milly did.

Riley hadn't cared. "Sure," he'd said. "Whatever you want."

What she'd wanted was him. And she'd been very willing when he tugged her shirt out of her jeans.

Now—in the middle of the convenience store with half of the community looking on—was not the time to remember that! Her face flamed.

"We're invited, of course," Ev said, oblivious, fortunately, to the direction of her thoughts. It wasn't a question.

Dori answered anyway. "You're all invited."

"Hear that," Ev announced to the store at large. "We're all invited to Dori and Riley's weddin'!"

There was the soft sound of a gasp behind them, and Dori turned to see Tricia Cannon staring at her, white-faced.

Dori felt her own color drain. She hadn't meant to announce their impending wedding quite like that. And especially not in front of Tricia.

"We haven't quite set the date yet," she told the other woman politely.

"Haven't you?" Tricia gave Dori a strained smile. Then she turned and, leaving a loaf of bread on the counter, walked out.

Riley almost didn't answer the phone.

It rarely rang for him, anyway. But he was in the house, and he thought it was Dori, calling from town, wanting to know if he'd thought of anything else she ought to pick up. There was no one else it could be.

So he grabbed it. "Hi, sweetheart. Miss me, do you?"

"Oh, I do, Riley. I do." It was a woman's voice. But it wasn't Dori.

He gulped. *"Trish?"*

There was a sniffle. "You were right," she said. "Absolutely right when you shoved me away. We shouldn't have done anything then. But it's different now, Riley. It's going to be different."

He unglued his tongue from the roof of his mouth. "What the hell are you talkin' about?"

"Us, Riley. You and me. You were the one for me all along. You saw it. I didn't." She was babbling.

He was confused. "Tricia, make sense."

"I am making sense, Riley." Her voice was urgent. "I've

never made more sense. It's just taken me forever. But I don't want you making the same mistake I made.''

''What? What are you talking about?''

''Marrying the wrong person! Taking second best. Don't do it, Riley.''

''Tricia—''

''You don't have to do it! I've made up my mind. I'm leaving here. I'm divorcing Jeff!''

''*What!*''

''I love you, Riley! I always have. I always will. And there's no sense in both of us being married to the wrong people. I'm leaving today. As soon as I pack. I'll call you from Denver.''

''Trish! No, you can't—''

''You said you wouldn't touch me when I was married, Riley.''

''I know. I—''

''I'm not going to be married anymore.'' She hung up.

And Riley stood staring at the receiver in his hand.


''Ev invited everybody to the wedding,'' Dori told him when she got home.

He was sitting in the kitchen at the table, staring at his hands. He looked…bereft, almost. As if someone had died. And when she spoke to him, she wasn't sure he heard a word she said.

Dori dumped the bags on the counter. ''It was insane the way they all knew what was going to happen before I told them. I think we have Jake to thank for that.''

Riley still looked blank. ''Huh?''

She looked at him more closely. He looked somewhat pale. ''Are you all right? Did you get hurt? What are you doing in the house?''

He seemed to come back from a long way away. He gave a small shake of his head. ''I came in to grab some lunch.''

Dori glanced at her watch. ''It's almost four.''

He stared at her but she didn't think he saw her. ''Uh-huh,'' he said. He didn't say anything else.

Her brow furrowed. ''What happened, Riley? It's not Jake?

Did something happen to Jake?'' She heard a shrill edge to her own voice.

Jake had gone to Maggie's again. She'd dropped him off on the way to town. Surely he would have said if Maggie had called!

"It's not...Jake.''

"Then...what?''

"It's Tricia,'' he said numbly.

Dori started. "Tricia? Why?'' She remembered the shocked look on the other woman's face. "Did she call to congratulate us?'' She gave Riley a wry smile and hoped he would smile, too.

He didn't. He didn't do anything. He just sat there, staring at something she couldn't see.

Then he said, "She's...getting a divorce.''

# Eleven

Tricia was free.

Oh, not yet…but she would be.

The one thing he'd hoped for—and had never admitted, even to himself—for the past dozen years was actually coming true.

Now.

*Why now?*

Why not before he'd met Dori Malone? Why not before he'd got involved with her and her son? Why not when he was still free himself instead of about to get married?

He couldn't believe it.

He played the conversation over in his mind, hearing her words again and again. *I love you, Riley. I always have. I always will. I don't want you to make the same mistake I did. Don't marry the wrong person.*

The words tumbled through his mind, made a whirl of his thoughts, a snarl of his emotions. *I love you, Riley. I'm not going to be married anymore…*

Damn. He sat on horseback staring down at the ranch house.

He could see Dori in the yard, pitching a ball to Jake. Jake swung and missed and landed on his butt in the dirt. Dori hauled him to his feet again, and they laughed and laughed.

It was a scene he'd dreamed about for years—of coming home and looking down and seeing his family there. For so long he'd been on the outside of other families, looking in.

But he didn't have to be on the outside of this one. Dori and Jake belonged at the ranch now. They were a part of it—a part of him.

And yet...Tricia still loved him.

*It doesn't matter,* he told himself fiercely. *It's past. Tricia's past.*

It didn't matter what she was doing now. He'd made a commitment. Riley kept his commitments—no matter what.

He drew a deep breath, touched his heels to the sorrel's sides and rode down to meet them.

Jake's face broke into a grin when he spotted his uncle coming down the hillside.

Dori was smiling, too, but her gaze was more serious. Probing, almost, as she looked at him. As if she knew his turmoil. But she couldn't. He hadn't said a word after he'd told her Tricia was getting a divorce. He never would.

It didn't matter. He wouldn't let it.

Jake came running. "Hooray, you're back! Now we can go get Tugger!"

Riley looked at Dori. She stayed where she was in the yard, but lifted her hand to shade her eyes as she looked up at him and nodded. "Maggie called and said the puppies were ready to go home."

"So can we?" Jake was jumping from one foot to the other. "Can we go now?"

Once upon a time Riley had dreamed of getting a dog for his kids. Only they hadn't been gangly dark-haired boys who looked like him but little towheaded urchins like their mother.

Would someone else get Tricia's kids a dog? Would someone else besides Jeff have children with her?

He shoved the thought away and cleared his throat. "Sure.

Why not?'' He gave himself a little shake and mustered a smile. ''Let's.''

The puppy was a distraction. It occupied all of Jake's attention and a good part of Dori's. It wriggled in Jake's arms, ran around on the ground, then came and snuggled against Riley. It was a persistent, tumbling, panting little black-and-white ball of fluff. He scratched its ears and was grateful to have something to focus on when Maggie said to them, ''Did you hear about Jeff and Tricia?''

There was a second's pause. Then Dori answered. ''We heard they're getting a divorce.''

Maggie nodded. ''She went to Denver, I heard. Just took off.'' She shook her head. ''Such a sad thing.'' She looked at Riley for comment.

He didn't say a word. He had nothing to say. He concentrated on scratching the ears of Tugger who was wiggling once more in Jake's arms.

Then, ''He's peein' on me,'' Jake yelped.

''Put him down,'' Maggie commanded.

And the moment passed. They talked about housebreaking. They talked about crates and puppy food. Tricia wasn't mentioned again.

But he thought about her.

He couldn't stop thinking about her.

Two days ago, after she'd hung up from telling him she was going to get a divorce, that she was going to Denver, he'd wondered if she'd really meant it, if she'd really leave.

Apparently she had.

And then he wondered if she would call him the way she said she would. He wondered what she'd say if she did.

He knew what he'd say...

What he *had* to say...

*It's too late, Tricia. I have other commitments.*

Chris had told her to go home, to get lost, to take their unborn child and go away.

"It isn't that I don't love you," he'd said in a moment of total self-delusion.

"What is it then?" Dori had said, tears stinging, a lump in her throat the size of Mount Everest. She'd waited for the great revelation while Chris had paced the room, scowling and looking furious and distracted.

Finally he'd shaken his head and, in doing so, come to a moment of clarity. "It's that I just…I just…*can't.*"

He couldn't. He wouldn't.

Riley could. Riley would.

Dori knew Riley would marry her because he'd said he would, just like he'd given half the ranch to Jake because it was the right thing to do, just like he hadn't had sex with Tricia when she was married to Jeff because it would have been wrong.

Riley did the right thing. No matter what it cost him.

But he didn't love her.

Not the way he loved Tricia.

Dori knew that. She knew it from the way he had grown so quiet since Tricia had called with her news. She knew it from the way he seemed distracted when either she or Jake talked to him, as if part of him was here, but most of him had gone to Denver.

With her.

But more than that, she knew it when he came to bed with her.

They hadn't made love many times. She didn't have a lot of experience to go by. But she knew when a man's mind was where his body was.

Riley wasn't there.

Oh, he loved her. In fact there was almost a desperation in his lovemaking now, as if he was trying to prove to himself that it would work. But the sweetness was gone. The focus was shattered.

His body was in hers.

But his heart was elsewhere.

She had hoped that things would be all right. She had tried

to pretend that Tricia's divorce wouldn't make any difference, because it would hurt so bad if things went wrong.

After all these years Dori had dared to dream again, to let herself open up to another human being besides her son, to wear her heart on her sleeve. She'd fallen in love with Riley Stratton—first as a dream, then as a man.

But she couldn't have him.

She knew that now, as she lay in bed next to him and watched him sigh in his sleep. He muttered and twisted as if in pain.

She knew his pain.

And she knew she couldn't marry a man who didn't love her.


"Why're we packin'?"

"Because we need to go visit Aunt Milly for a while." Dori didn't turn to look at Jake when she answered him. She didn't want to see the surprised look in his eyes. She didn't want to see the worry, the hurt, the confusion.

"How come?"

"Because she invited us. I put your duffel bag on the bottom bunk. Go put in it what you want to take. We'll get the rest—" She broke off. "Just put in it what you want." She wasn't going to tell him they were leaving for good. She couldn't deal with that. Not yet.

"Don't wanta take anything. Don't wanta go," Jake said. "You go see Aunt Milly. I'll stay with Uncle Riley."

"No, dear. Grandma and Grandpa want to see you, too. They miss you." Not that she'd told them she was coming. She'd only called Milly this morning.

"Don't mention this to Mom and Dad," she'd said. "I just need a bolt hole. I'll find something. I just need a little time…and space."

"Are you sure about this?" Milly had demanded. "I thought you loved him."

"I—" Dori had been going to deny it, but she couldn't. "It won't work," she'd told Milly. "He doesn't love me."

That part Milly understood. She didn't argue anymore.

"We're takin' Tugger," Jake said. He wasn't asking.

"We'll take Tugger." Knowing that Tugger was coming along was going to be what got Jake out the door. "Go pack your bag and put it by the door. Then get Tugger's food and his crate."

"We're goin' now?" Jake clearly didn't think much of that.

"Now," Dori said.

She'd put it off, had dared to hope, but she couldn't hope now. Not after Tricia had called at lunchtime from Denver.

"Tell Riley I called," she'd said, her voice husky. From crying, Dori had wondered. She'd felt like crying herself.

"Yes," she'd said hollowly.

"Tell him I'll call back later," Tricia instructed.

"Yes," Dori agreed. But she wasn't going to wait around to tell him. She wasn't going to wait around to say goodbye. She knew Riley Stratton. He'd tell her that Tricia didn't matter, that he'd already committed himself to marry her.

Dori didn't need that kind of sacrifice.

She needed to get out of there while Riley was still gone.

"Come on, Jake," she urged. "I want to have some time to drive while it's still daylight."

Jake scowled, but finally he left.

Dori ended up helping him pack. They'd have been there hours if she'd waited for him to do it on his own. She threw his things in haphazardly, trying not to look at the picture of Riley and Tricia in high school prom garb, which was tacked to the bulletin board on the wall. She tried not to see Riley's shirt hanging on the doorknob, or his scuffed moccasins peeking out from under the bed.

She tried not to think about Riley.

But Riley was everywhere.

She lugged the duffels out to the car. She stowed them in the trunk. She put Tugger's crate in the back and started to put Tugger in it.

"He can't ride there. He's gotta ride with me!" Jake protested.

"He'll pee on you," Dori reminded him.

But Jake clutched the puppy against his chest. "I don't care."

"Fine. Let him pee on you." It was the least of her concerns. She blinked fiercely against tears and swallowed hard. She opened the front door and waited. "Just get in. Now."

"How come we're not waitin' to say goodbye to Uncle Riley?"

"I left him a note."

"But—"

"Jake, get in this car."

Jake got in the car. Dori breathed a sigh of relief. But when she came around to get in the other side, he had another question.

"Is Uncle Riley throwin' us out?"

She looked at Jake, startled. He was looking at her in complete seriousness, his eyes wide and worried as he regarded her over Tugger's head. "No, Jake. Of course not."

"Then why—"

"I told you. Aunt Milly—"

"This isn't about Aunt Milly."

"All right," Dori agreed, defeated. "It isn't about Aunt Milly. It's about your Uncle Riley and…and me. We were going to get married. Now we aren't. And the rest of it you're too young to understand!"

"I am not!" Jake said, indignant.

"Well, how about I'm too miserable to explain it to you, then?" Which was only the truth. More honesty. Poor Jake.

She sniffled and scrubbed at her eyes with her shirtsleeve. Then she started the engine, crashed the gears and stomped on the gas pedal, scattering gravel and sending the car shooting up the road.

Jake sat beside her silently, Tugger in his lap. He had, she was grateful to notice, stopped asking questions at last.

They weren't in the yard when he came over the rise.

The car wasn't beside the house. He supposed they'd gone

into town. Dori had said something about getting Jake school clothes, that he'd grown out of all his old ones. Riley could believe that. The boy seemed to have grown inches in the few weeks he'd been here. Once already Riley had even lengthened Jake's stirrups.

"He's outgrowin' everything," he'd said last night.

"He can't help it," Dori had replied, as if he'd been complaining.

He didn't complain. Ever. He just…endured.

Now he turned out his horse and went to check on Tugger. He whistled as he approached the pen he'd built by the side of the house, but Tugger didn't come running. Probably they'd taken him with them into town. Wherever Jake went, Tugger went, too.

He was sure he'd hear how taking the puppy shopping for school clothes went when they got home. He went up the steps, took off his boots and went into the house.

It felt quiet. Too quiet.

Of course it was quiet. They were in town.

He glanced at the table and saw a note there. Idly he picked it up and started to read.

As he read the words Dori had written, the bottom seemed to drop out of his world.

Dear Riley,
We have gone back to Livingston—not to my parents'. We'll be staying with my sister for a while. I'll be in touch when I know where we'll be and can arrange for our things to be shipped. I don't know yet about selling you the ranch. I think Jake may want to hang on to it, and I really can't tell him not to. But I can set you free to marry the woman you love. She called. She's in Denver. She'll call you later this afternoon.

Dori.

P.S. We've taken Tugger.

He'd barely finished reading it when the phone rang. With nerveless fingers, he grabbed it. "Dori?"

"N-no," a startled female voice replied. "It's Tricia."

Tricia.

"I called you earlier," she said, her voice husky. "I left a message."

"I got it."

She made a tremulous sound, somewhere between a sob and laugh. "Then you know I'm here. I'm settled. Well, not really settled. I have an apartment. I'm looking for a job. I've talked to Jeff about having the children with me part of the time when things are…calmer. I think it would be better for me to be here for a while before we talk about me coming back to the ranch. It's such a small town. You know how they talk."

"I know how they talk." He could barely get the words out. His mind was reeling.

"And maybe you'll like it here well enough to decide you don't want that ranch after all. You were going to leave it once, remember?"

He remembered that she'd thought he would leave it. He hadn't denied it. He'd taken the easy way out. He'd remained silent and let her believe what she wanted to believe.

She went on now. "You'll like Denver. It's a long drive, but not terrible. We can have weekends. And then maybe by the time we get married you'll want to move here. What do you think?"

*By the time we get married…*

There it was. His heart's desire. The relationship he'd always wanted with the one woman he'd always loved.

But she wasn't the woman he loved.

Not the way he loved Dori Malone.

He knew it then, recognized it at last, saw that his youthful infatuation with Tricia had been just that. It had revved his hormones, made his body come to attention, plucked the strings of his emotions, played havoc with his pride.

But what he felt for Tricia had never hit the core of him. It had never touched his heart.

Dori had touched his heart.

Her stubborn refusal to let Jake's dreams be trampled, her determined commitment to making a home for them on the ranch, her curtain making, her painting, her computer skills, her laughing, her teasing, her wondrous lovemaking—all of it Riley loved. There wasn't a selfish bone in her body. She was as giving and loving as Tricia was selfish. And finally Riley understood that.

"Riley? I only said you *might* want to move here," Tricia began.

"No."

"Well, if you don't, we can talk about it, I guess, but—"

"I'm not coming to Denver, Tricia. I'm not…marrying you."

There was a moment's stunned silence. "Don't tell me you're going to honor your commitment to her now! Honestly, Riley—"

"She isn't here. She left me."

"Well, then—"

"I love her, Trish. I love *her!*" Maybe it was the wrong thing to say. Certainly it wasn't a very tactful thing to say. But Riley had never been long on tact. Or patience.

"But—"

"I gotta go, Trish! You divorce Jeff if you want, but don't you divorce him for me. I'm marryin' Dori—if she'll have me."

Then he banged down the phone. He didn't know how much of a head start she had, but he knew he had to catch her.

Jake had never made a call from a pay phone before.

He wasn't sure how to do it, so he asked the checkout girl in the gas station. She didn't know much, either, because she was only about sixteen and too busy flirting with a couple of rodeo cowboys to pay much attention to him. But one of the cowboys knew how.

"You wanta reverse the charges," he told Jake. "That means the other guy pays for the call."

"Sounds good." Jake glanced over his shoulder, hoping his

mother couldn't see him. She thought he was in the men's room while she was in the women's.

"I'll show you," the cowboy said. "What's the number?"

Jake told him. The cowboy punched it in. "When they answer, the operator will ask if they'll accept a collect call from…and you say your name." The cowboy grinned. "That's all there is to it."

Jake wished that was the truth.

The phone rang and rang. And just when he was about to give up, he heard his uncle's voice. "Dori?"

"No, it's—"

But the operator cut in. "I have a collect call from…"

There was a second of dead silence. Then Jake remembered what the cowboy had told him. "Jake! It's me, Uncle Riley! I—"

"Do you accept the—"

"Yes, damn it! Jake, where are you?"

"In a gas station. We're gettin' gas. We're goin' to Aunt Milly's. What'd you do to my mom?"

"Nothing! I didn't do anything. I didn't want you to leave. Hell, I—*Jake, where are you?*"

Jake looked around. One gas station looked like any other to him. "Hey," he said to the cowboys who were still chatting to the checkout girl. "Where are we?"

They looked at him, then at each other. They shrugged.

The checkout girl popped her gum. "Ranchester," she told them all.

Jake repeated that to his uncle.

"Right. I can be there in a couple of hours. Stay put," Uncle Riley said.

"Mom won't," Jake told him. "She doesn't know I called you. If she finds out, she'll leave."

Uncle Riley muttered something on the other end of the line.

"What?" Jake said. He'd never heard Uncle Riley use words like that before.

"You gotta stop her," Uncle Riley said. "Disable the car."

"Disable the car?" Jake repeated doubtfully.

"She can't leave if you disable the car. Let the air out of tires."

Jake's eyes widened a little. "How?" he asked a little breathless.

Uncle Riley told him. Then he said, "It might not take her long to get 'em pumped again. You might have to do something else. You could pull the boots off the tops of the spark plugs."

"She might notice me foolin' around under the hood."

"Right. Well, then—"

"She's comin'," Jake blurted. "I gotta go."

"Keep her there," Uncle Riley said. "I'll be there as quick as I can. Just keep her there. Do that for me, can you, Jake?"

"Can a bear climb trees? That's what Grandpa always said."

Uncle Riley almost laughed. "Go for it, son."

It wasn't easy. There were too darn many helpful cowboys and truckers around willing to help a lady in distress. And Jake's mom, even red-eyed from crying, seemed to be a magnet for most of them.

Jake let the air out. They pumped it up. He needed to go to the bathroom. He lobbied for dinner.

"I'm starvin'," he told her. He ate as slowly as he could. He ate more than he'd eaten in his life. He thought he'd probably bust. He hoped to heck Uncle Riley hurried up.

"Come on, Jake," his mother urged. "Aunt Milly's expecting us."

"We could spend the night here."

"We're not spending the night here. Come on." She hauled him back to the car and reluctantly he climbed in. His mother went around and started the car.

"I gotta go to the bathroom again," Jake blurted. "An' so does Tugger."

"Fine. Go to the bathroom. Hurry up. And while you're there, I'll take Tugger into the lot." She switched off the ignition and got out, taking Tugger on his leash with her.

Jake waited until she was gone, then he ambled to the bathroom. He came back almost at once, and when his mother returned, he was waiting for her.

"Any more reasons to stall?" she asked him.

He shook his head.

She reached to turn on the key. It wasn't there. She looked in her purse, on the seat of the car, in her jacket pocket.

"What did I do with the key?" she asked Jake.

Jake shook his head. "I don't know."

"Oh, good grief." His mother almost banged her head on the steering wheel. "Go inside and see if I left the keys on the counter. I'll look out here."

"Okay." Jake bounced out of the car.

"I have to find the key. What could I have done with it?"

He was almost afraid she'd start crying again. He was pretty sure *he'd* be the one crying if she ever found out he'd flushed the key down the toilet.


Riley saw her car as he approached the gas station. He'd driven like a bat out of hell all the way to Ranchester, praying he wasn't ticketed. He was.

Twice.

He didn't care. He only wanted to get to Dori.

And now that he saw her there, surrounded by a half-dozen ranchers, truckers and cowboys, all looking worried and concerned, all fussing over her, he turned the corner before he pulled to a stop.

No one noticed him. No one except Jake.

The boy was sitting on a bench by the station, holding Tugger in his lap. When he spied Riley's truck, he got up. But he didn't come toward him when Riley got out of the truck. He just held Tugger and watched.

Waited.

For Riley to do what he needed to do.

It wasn't the scene Riley would have chosen. He hated an audience. He had a big one. He hated to see women cry. He could hear Dori sniffling now.

"It's just…been a hard day," he heard her tell the assembled truckers and cowboys. "D-don't mind me."

There was rustling and muttering among them. "Anything we can do for you, ma'am," and "Sure do wish we could find that key," and "Reckon I'll just go wake that locksmith."

And he figured they'd be there forever, helping, unless he stepped in.

He cleared his throat. "Dori?"

She jerked around. The men all fell silent as she stared at him. For one instant her gaze sought Jake's. He stood there, hugging Tugger against his chest. He swallowed, and then he nodded, but he didn't look away.

Whatever passed between mother and son, her gaze came back to Riley. She was crying again.

"I suppose you came to help," she said.

"No."

She looked startled. "No?"

Slowly he shook his head. "I came because I love you."

She just stared at him.

It wasn't the first time in his life he'd wished for Chris's smooth words and easy charm. But it wasn't him. Never had been.

"Tricia," she began at last.

"Called," he finished for her. "She's in Denver. She invited me to Denver. I don't want to go. I held on to that dream for years without even realizing I didn't want it anymore. I don't love Tricia, Dori. I love you." His voice was ragged. His words were awkward. He was as bad at this feelings stuff as he'd always thought he'd be. And to have to say it all in front of an audience didn't bear thinking about.

But at least Dori was listening. "You…love *me?*"

"You. And Jake." There was no way he could leave Jake out of this. "And I reckon I'll find room for Tugger, too."

As he spoke he felt more than saw Jake come to stand beside him. The two of them stood side by side, looking at Dori.

"You're the one—the ones—I want," he went on doggedly.

He put a hand on Jake's shoulder. "I'm no prize, Dori. But I do love you. Come home. Marry me. Please."

And then Dori threw her arms around him.

"Yes," she whispered against his mouth. "Yes. Oh, Riley, yes. I'll marry you."

A loud burst of applause and cheers sounded behind her. Riley barely noticed. He certainly didn't care.

He only cared about Dori. And Jake. And Tugger.

And the future they would make together.

He gathered them all into his arms and knew the joy that came from being part of a family, from finding dreams mended he'd thought long broken, but mostly from finding the woman—and the boy—he would forever be able to call his own.

"How did you find us?" she asked him when at last they were home and Jake had been tucked up in bed.

"Jake called me."

"Jake?" She was astonished, and yet she wasn't. She remembered the sudden tire problem, the stalling, the missing key. "Jake." Her gaze narrowed. She started toward the bedroom.

Riley grabbed her back. "Let the boy sleep. Thank him tomorrow."

"I wasn't going to thank him," Dori said tartly. "What do you suppose he did with that key?"

"I haven't a clue," Riley said. "I don't care. Meeting the locksmith in Ranchester tomorrow is a small price to pay for getting you back." He kissed her again.

She loved his kisses. Mere hours ago she never thought she'd kiss him again.

"Are you sure?" she asked him now. "Really sure? Tricia—"

He put a finger against her mouth. "I told you. Tricia is past. I think she was probably past a long, long time ago. I was just too fixated to realize it. You gave me my shot at Tricia, you stubborn woman. I don't want her. I only want you."

And she believed him now. Riley Stratton didn't lie. He didn't cheat. He didn't do anything wrong. Ever.

"You're perfect," she told him.

He laughed out loud. "We'll see how long you believe that, sweetheart."

"I love you," Dori told him. "You're perfect for me."

And Riley grinned again. "I'll settle for that."


"We're home," Jake told Tugger drowsily as they burrowed down in the bed. It was the middle of the night. They were both exhausted. Tugger had had an accident in Riley's truck on the way home, but Riley hadn't cared.

"Reckon it'll be the first of many," he'd said, and he'd ruffled Jake's hair.

Jake had thought maybe then would be a good time to tell them about the key in the toilet. His mom probably wouldn't get too mad. Riley might even get him another puppy. Or maybe, down the road, they'd agree to a brother or sister. Jared seemed to have fun with his. Jake thought he might like one, too.

"We'll have to talk to 'em about it," he told Tugger who wasn't supposed to be in bed with him, but his mom and Uncle Riley hadn't noticed. They'd only been looking at each other.

Jake was pleased. And he was pushing his luck tonight. "You're gonna stay right here," he told the puppy.

Now he pushed himself up to where he could look out the window at a night sky awash with stars. He cradled the pup in his arms. There were a lot of stars out there—millions, his mom said. Enough for everybody.

Enough for everybody's dreams.

He thought about his father, about his mom and Uncle Riley, about the stardust cowboy, about dreams. He thought about his grandpa and wished his grandpa believed just a little in stardust.

Jake could have told him it worked.

He picked out one particular star and said, "You might try to convince him."

It wouldn't hurt. Maybe the stardust cowboy could work miracles, too.

He sure did make dreams come true.

"It's been a terrific adventure so far," Jake said softly, his eyes on the heavens. "An' now that we're here for good, I reckon we'll have lots more. An' you'll always be a part of it," he promised. "You an' Mom an' Riley an' Tugger an' me."

Then with starlight falling on him and Tugger tucked under his chin, Jake snuggled down under the covers and slept.

\* \* \* \* \*

*Harvard-educated lawyer/cowboy Rance Phillips has more women than he knows what to do with. He can have any woman—it seems—except the one woman he wants! Will he get her? Find out in COWBOY ON THE RUN, a CODE OF THE WEST title, coming soon from Silhouette's World's Most Eligible Bachelors.*

**SILHOUETTE®**

*Desire*

**A hidden passion, a hidden child,
a hidden fortune.**

**Revel in the unfolding of these
powerful, passionate…**

*SECRETS!*

**A brand-new miniseries from
Silhouette Desire® author**

# Barbara McCauley

July 1999
**BLACKHAWK'S SWEET REVENGE** (SD #1230)
Lucas Blackhawk wanted revenge! And by marrying
Julianna Hadley, he would finally have it. Was exacting
revenge worth losing this new but true love?

August 1999
**SECRET BABY SANTOS** (SD #1236)
She had never meant to withhold the truth from **Nick Santos**,
but when Maggie Smith found herself alone and pregnant, she
had been unable to face the father of her child. Now Nick was
back—and determined to discover what secrets Maggie was
keeping.…

September 1999
**KILLIAN'S PASSION** (SD #1242)
**Killian Shawnessey** had been on his own since childhood.
So when Cara Sinclair showed up in his life claiming he had
a family—and had inherited millions—Killian vowed to keep
his loner status. Would Cara be able to convince Killian that
his empty future could be filled by a shared love?

*Secrets!* available at your favorite retail outlet store.

**Silhouette®**

SDSRT

If you enjoyed what you just read,
then we've got an offer you can't resist!

# Take 2 bestselling love stories FREE!

# Plus get a FREE surprise gift!

---

**Clip this page and mail it to Silhouette Reader Service™**

| IN U.S.A. | IN CANADA |
|---|---|
| 3010 Walden Ave. | P.O. Box 609 |
| P.O. Box 1867 | Fort Erie, Ontario |
| Buffalo, N.Y. 14240-1867 | L2A 5X3 |

**YES!** Please send me 2 free Silhouette Desire® novels and my free surprise gift. Then send me 6 brand-new novels every month, which I will receive months before they're available in stores. In the U.S.A., bill me at the bargain price of $3.12 plus 25¢ delivery per book and applicable sales tax, if any*. In Canada, bill me at the bargain price of $3.49 plus 25¢ delivery per book and applicable taxes**. That's the complete price and a savings of over 10% off the cover prices—what a great deal! I understand that accepting the 2 free books and gift places me under no obligation ever to buy any books. I can always return a shipment and cancel at any time. Even if I never buy another book from Silhouette, the 2 free books and gift are mine to keep forever. So why not take us up on our invitation. You'll be glad you did!

225 SEN CNFA
326 SEN CNFC

| Name | (PLEASE PRINT) | |
|---|---|---|
| Address | Apt.# | |
| City | State/Prov. | Zip/Postal Code |

 * Terms and prices subject to change without notice. Sales tax applicable in N.Y.
** Canadian residents will be charged applicable provincial taxes and GST.
   All orders subject to approval. Offer limited to one per household.
   ® are registered trademarks of Harlequin Enterprises Limited.

DES99                                                    ©1998 Harlequin Enterprises Limited

# Silhouette® SPECIAL EDITION®
## AND SILHOUETTE®
### Desire®
### The Bachelor Bet

*In bestselling author **Joan Elliott Pickart's** engaging new series, three bachelor friends have bet that marriage and family will never be a part of their lives. But they'll learn never to bet against love....*

## TAMING TALL, DARK BRANDON
### Desire #1223, June 1999
**Brandon Hamilton** had long ago given up on the idea of home, hearth and babies. But when he meets stubborn beauty Andrea Cunningham, he finds himself in danger of being thoroughly and irrevocably tamed....

## THE IRRESISTIBLE MR. SINCLAIR
### Special Edition #1256, July 1999
**Taylor Sinclair** believes marriage is for fools, but he reconsiders when he falls for Janice Jennings—a secretly stunning woman who hides behind a frumpy disguise. A barrier Taylor vows to breach...

## THE MOST ELIGIBLE M.D.
### Special Edition #1262, August 1999
She's a woman without a past. He's a man without a future. Still, **Dr. Ben Rizzoli** cannot quell his passion for the delicate amnesiac who's made him live and love—and long for the family he believes he can never have....

*Don't miss **Joan Elliott Pickart's** newest series, **The Bachelor Bet**— in Silhouette Desire and Silhouette Special Edition!*
Available at your favorite retail outlet.

### Silhouette®

SDTBB

*This June 1999, the legend
continues in Jacobsville*

# Diana Palmer

## LONG, TALL TEXANS
### EMMETT, REGAN & BURKE

This June 1999, Silhouette brings readers
an extra-special trade-size collection
for Diana Palmer's legion of fans.
These three favorite Long, Tall Texans
stories have been brought back in
one collectible trade-size edition.

*Emmett, Regan & Burke are about to be led
down the bridal path by three irresistible women.
Get ready for the fireworks!*

Don't miss this collection of favorite
Long, Tall Texans stories...
**available in June 1999**
at your favorite retail outlet.

Then in August 1999 watch for
LOVE WITH A LONG, TALL TEXAN
a trio of brand-new short stories featuring
three irresistible Long, Tall Texans.

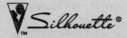

# COMING NEXT MONTH

**#1225 PRINCE CHARMING'S CHILD—Jennifer Greene**
*10th Anniversary Man of the Month/Happily Ever After*
Pregnant? Impossible! Nicole Stewart knew she hadn't done *anything* that could get her pregnant! Of course, she did have some passionate memories of being in handsome architect Mitch Landers's strong arms.... But that had been a dream...right?

**#1226 LOVERS' REUNION—Anne Marie Winston**
Explorer Marco Esposito's knee—and career—were shot, but he was determined to discover new territories again. Then beauty Sophie Morrell walked back into his life. Sophie had always loved Marco, but could she convince him that *she* was his most exciting rediscovery?

**#1227 THAT McCLOUD WOMAN—Peggy Moreland**
*Texas Brides*
He was determined to protect his heart. Jack Cordell had been hurt deeply once, and even though he was attracted to lovely Alayna McCloud, he would never again bare his soul to another. It was up to Alayna to show Jack that with love anything is possible....

**#1228 THE SHEIK'S SECRET—Judith McWilliams**
Being mistaken for his twin brother was the plan. Falling in love with his brother's ex-fiancée *wasn't!* Yet how could Sheik Hassan Rashid resist Kali Whitman's tempting sensuality? But would Kali's love endure once she learned Hassan was not the man he claimed to be?

**#1229 PLAIN JANE'S TEXAN—Jan Hudson**
It was love at first sight. At least for millionaire Matt Crow. But plain-Jane Eve Ellison needed some convincing. So Matt sat down in his boardroom to plan a campaign to win her heart. But Eve had other ideas...and they didn't involve a boardroom....

**#1230 BLACKHAWK'S SWEET REVENGE—Barbara McCauley**
*Secrets!*
Lucas Blackhawk wanted revenge! And by marrying Julianna Hadley, he would finally have it. But Lucas soon discovered that sweet Julianna was nothing like her cold family. Was exacting revenge worth losing this new but true love?